Tsk. Tsk. I see you, but do you see me?

Prepare yourself for a journey into the intriguing world of the Savin Brothers Bratva. It's bound to be emotional, intense, and a little chaotic. But don't fret. I'll be right by your side to protect you from harm, even if you don't realize I'm there.

Now, be a good girl and turn the page...

NOTE TO READERS

This book contains violent and spicy romance scenes that may not be suitable for all readers. 18+ only.

READING ORDER

<u>The Savin Brothers Bratva Romance</u>

Prequel: Promised to Me
Book One: Deadly Decisions
Book Two: A Love That Bleeds
Book Three: Gameplay

CONTENTS

1. Elise Walsh — 1

2. Dmitri Savin — 9

3. Dmitri — 15

4. Elise — 23

5. Elise — 29

6. Elise — 37

7. Andrei Savin — 45

8. Dmitri — 55

9. Elise — 61

10. Dmitri — 69

11. Elise — 75

12. Elise — 81

13. Dmitri — 87

14. Elise — 97

15. Elise — 101

16. Dmitri — 107

17. Elise — 113

18. Elise — 119

19. Elise   123

20. Dmitri   131

21. Elise   139

22. Dmitri   145

23. Elise   153

24. Dmitri   159

25. Dmitri   163

26. Dmitri   169

27. Elise   173

28. Dmitri   177

29. Elise   181

30. Dmitri   185

31. Andrei   187

32. Dmitri   191

33. Elise   195

34. Elise   201

A NOTE FROM THE AUTHOR   205

CONTINUE READING   207

Chapter One

ELISE WALSH

The gun weighs a little in my hand, almost as though it senses my impatience.

"So, why is Dmitri in town?" I ask, standing above the man who is down on his knees and looking up at me. His eyes twitch a few times, and his throat bobbles. He is trying to remain calm, his gaze shifting to the gun now and then, and the beads of sweat give his face a dull shimmer.

"I don't know, Ms. Elise. I promise," he says with a shaking voice.

Moving my finger around the gun, I shake my head and narrow my eyes, then repeat my question, this time letting the words come out slowly. "Viktor, why is Dmitri back in town?"

Viktor closes his eyes and exhales deeply, muttering some inaudible curse. "The brothers aren't saying. He showed up at El Grande, and no one's saying why."

I hold my gun to Viktor's head. "Viktor, if you don't know, then you're useless to me."

His eyes widen, panic filling his voice. He sputters the words quickly, stumbling over them a few times. It makes me grimace. "Ms. Elise, I swear if I knew, I would tell you."

Viktor surveys around the room as the cartel men stand, watching him on his knees, begging for his life. A deadly silence drapes over the room, only cut occasionally by the shifting of boots and Viktor's frantic, helpless panting.

"Viktor, it's okay. Thank you for the information. You can go home now."

Relief washes over his face, but only for a second. He looks at me closely again as if trying to decipher my emotions. I show none. He glances at the men around the room, licks his dry lips, and exhales a few times. "Thanks, Ms. Elise. I swear I'll call you immediately if I hear anything else."

"I know you will." I give Viktor my hand and help him to his feet. "Goodnight, Viktor."

With a wary smile, he says his goodbyes. "Goodnight."

Viktor slowly moves to the exit door. I wave at him, still smiling, then transition my wave to a beckoning call to Diego.

Diego steps forward, and I hand the gun over to him.

He's poker-faced when he raises his hand, pointing the weapon at the back of Viktor's head.

A bang rips through the air, punctuating the silence with death's grim finality, and a loud grunt is followed by a heavy thud. Viktor slams onto the ground, followed shortly by the stench of iron pervading the air as redness coats the walls and ceiling, trickling down. It is like some macabre modern artwork in a gallery, painting pristine white walls.

My lips purse. Now my inside informant is dead, I'll have to find someone new to give me information about the happenings of the Russian Bratva.

Picking up my tablet, I find myself naturally staring at the pictures of the most handsome man I've ever seen; a brutal man, a Russian. His black hair is as dark as the hell from which he has crawled, but his angelic hazel eyes give him a softness. The way he stands and the veins on his wrist show how muscular he is, while an expensive suit and a watch valued at more than my car describe a dangerous man to whom I should not be attracted to.

Yet I am.

"Are you going to stare at that file all night?"

Liam's voice springs up, and he's watching me with the intensity of a pair of eyes trying to see into someone's mind, read it, and decipher someone else's hidden code. He leans against a wall, arms folded as ever. He is always watching, waiting to see what I'm thinking, making me second-guess myself. But I'm a young woman who can feign being emotionless whenever I choose not to show what I feel.

I glance up at him, barely. "Nope," I reply.

His lips stretch to the side, and he scoffs. I'm pretty sure the cartel prince just caught me staring at Dmitri, biting my lower lip.

I move quickly past Viktor's body, lying in a crumpled mess on the floor, covered in crimson, and rush out the door before Liam can see the flush of red on my face. The last thing I need is for my boss and head of the cartel to catch me in my attraction to the enemy, a Bratva boss.

My assistant Jessica enters my office behind me with a cautious tone. "Should I get you coffee?"

I touch my face, still warm and blushing, the image remaining in my head as if imprinted there, the vision of how those hazel eyes seem to peer at one's soul. A shudder passes through me, top to toe, before I noisily clear my throat, cheeks still far too pink.

Jessica stands patiently, waiting.

"Always coffee, Jessica," I mutter.

As she exits my office, I open the tablet again and stare at the file given to me. *Dmitri Savin, why are you back in New York? Why now?*

Jessica walks back into the office with my extra hot vanilla latte. The creamy smell fills the air, comforting me.

"What or who has you smiling like that, Elise?" Jessica chuckles.

"Nothing. Absolutely nothing. Why don't you call it a night, and I'll see you tomorrow." It is not a question, more of a mandate.

Jessica turns to leave. "See you tomorrow," she says and walks out.

I laugh, whispering, "Nosy bitch" into the now quiet office air. If anyone knows me, it's her. Having been my assistant for the past few years, she knows if something or someone has caught my attention. Not a fiber of my body can deny that someone has, indeed, caught my focus.

So, here again, alone, so late… Why am I the last one in the office at ten o'clock? But I'm always the last one here and the first in the door in the mornings.

Right now, most of the men are at the gentleman's club or some hotel having a glass of tequila with a woman or a few women, ready to service them when they snap their fingers. They'll show up sometime tomorrow, before lunch, hungover and coming down from tonight's blow. But I must earn their respect by working three times harder than any of them.

A shitty deal, but it's worth it.

Today, I'm the youngest and highest-ranking female in the Martinez Cartel and the Chief Operating Officer of various tequila bars on the East Coast. Of course, these are all fronts through which to launder our drug money.

Hmm, Dmitri Savin.

An hour ago, I wouldn't even have cared about him! No, not a care in the world, not sparing a solitary thought for him, not even letting his name flit momentarily through my mind. So, why now? Because now, he is my new assignment and—equally, it seems—my brand-new obsession, setting my heart thumping while hot blood flows through my veins.

His image flashes through my head again, forceful and intrusive.

So, Dmitri … You have piqued my interest. How dare you invade my thoughts in this way? Who told you that you could?

I chuckle. If only it were that easy to forbid him to enter my mind!

Dmitri is the second eldest Savin brother. After their father died, the five brothers continued their family's legacy and billion-dollar fortune. For the past three years, Dmitri has been running their family's operations in Russia. His eldest brother, Andrei—also known as the Brigadier—has been running the U.S. operations out of New York. Andrei is a crucial player in my new deal, which is almost finalized.

When I started working for the cartel, I studied all the New York players. The Savin brothers were the first on my list to learn about. They were famous for being young, successful, and some of the cruelest men one could ever encounter. Nothing has changed in the interim.

Standing up, I walk back and forth across my office. Andrei has assured me the Savins have approved my deal, but there's a reason Dmitri is in town unexpectedly. If Andrei were to pull out of the negotiations, the deal would be dead. And so would my career.

Anxiously striding out of the office, I head downstairs to a heavily patronized tequila bar. Our corporate offices are on the second floor of one of our New Jersey locations. At this time on a Friday night, the bar is packed with young college kids spending Daddy's money and middle-aged men and women trying to celebrate the end of the week by frittering away their paychecks.

Quickly, I push and shove my way through the milling throng to make my way to the back door, waving to the two bartenders pouring tequila flights for a half-drunken crowd.

"Where to?" Alejandro asks as he quickly runs to the back passenger door of my new SUV, which is black, bulletproof, and, of course, fully paid for by the cartel.

"New York City," I say, my face still buried in the file.

"At this hour?" He closes the door.

"Yes. There's something I want to check on tonight." He knows me, knows that I work until the early morning hours. But even so, I usually don't take midnight drives between New York and New Jersey. This instance is something of an anomaly, let's say.

"Okay, Elise." He slips into the driver's seat and starts heading to the city that never sleeps.

I haven't dated or been with a man since joining the cartel. It makes for lonely Friday nights, during which I comfort my loneliness by diving into work. You can't focus on cravings when there's important work to do and not much time to do it. But some nights, the loneliness becomes overwhelming, wishing there could be someone with whom to share an exciting win or a terrible loss.

The men in this business are plentiful, bringing a lot of advances my way. However, the minute I take one of them up on their offer, other players will invariably assume that's how I've become successful. Only very few women are high-ranking in the underground world. In a world in which women are viewed only as wives and property, it's hard for us ladies to get ahead without judgment. So, it's better not to risk affecting their perception of me.

But thankfully, times are changing at last. The traditional men in this life are either dying or retiring, and the new leadership of younger men, such as Liam and Andrei, recognize our worth. It's a gradual shift, but at least it's changing. I'm happy to be one of the few women pioneering growth in this line of work. Still, it's an unfair game in the cartel.

Right now, my priorities are all too clear, and a man doesn't rank among them. That said, my trusted friend awaits on my nightstand to keep me happy. With my preferred vibrator always charged and ready to please, who needs the headaches a man would bring into my life?

We are about a block from El Grande, but why did I come this way?

El Grande is a beautiful tower in New York City owned by the Coalition, the most powerful Bratva in the world. The tenants are all members of the Coalition and associates.

Only with the Coalition's approval can tenants sell their overpriced condominiums, although even then, they may do so only to other members.

The condominiums are exclusive, with heavily armored security around the building and on its rooftop. In fact, a source informs me the Savin brothers occupy the fifty-sixth floor of El Grande, just one floor below the Pakhan's penthouse.

"Are you sure you want to drive by El Grande, Elise?" Alejandro cautiously slows, fully alert. His hands clutch the wheel, his eyes darting to the rearview mirror several times.

"Yes, Alejandro. We're just driving by. We'll be fine."

Driving past El Grande, it is midnight, and things inside are quiet and dark. Of course, there are always snipers unseen but ready on the rooftop and over a thousand cameras strategically positioned around. They whirl and buzz, humming as they pivot to follow the view of the cars and any movements occurring down below in the streets.

My eyes pass the front doors to the empty sidewalk with just one lonely pedestrian. *Wait! Is that Dmitri walking down the street?*

My body bolts upright, eyes fixing on the man outside. I tap the back of the driver's seat with urgency. "Alejandro, follow that man, but not too close."

"Yes, Elise." His voice is cautious, laced with a sprinkling of doubt. But he obeys, wordless beyond a small show of acquiescence.

Three blocks away, Dmitri enters a small, dimly lit bar that is surprisingly empty for a Friday night.

"Stop!" I order Alejandro as he pulls the SUV to the side of the street. "I'll be right back." And before he can stop me, my feet are alighting onto the sidewalk, stepping as quietly as I can.

Frigid air brushes against my skin as I rush to the door, pausing before walking into the bar. Surely, I should turn around and head home. But I can't because he is right there, the man over whom I've been obsessing for the last few hours. He is in there, and I must get closer.

Chapter Two

DMITRI SAVIN

Staring out of the window walls of my El Grande condo, New York City looks bright and full of life. Its twinkling lights flash and sparkle, dotting the horizon like a million fireflies. I miss the vibrant and effervescent New York energy, and most of all, I miss my family.

Don't get me wrong, Russia had its moments. And in Russia, where the rules don't apply to the Coalition, I have had my share of fun these past three years. But I'm home now. Andrei has asked that I return and start running the family's U.S. operations alongside him. We have enough managers, accountants, and lawyers to run our businesses in Russia. Frequent trips there will ensure everything continues running smoothly.

Arriving home a few hours ago, I got straight to work. "Robert, the Brigadier has asked you a question," I say, looking away from the bright city to the Irishman sitting poised like a coiled spring, taut and fractious, on the folding chair in the middle of my living room.

"Fuck yourself, you Russian bastard," he growls, spitting at me. Luckily, I'm light on my feet, darting a step back before it comes to land on my new shoes.

"Guess it's my lucky day, motherfucker." Grinning, I take a step forward, fist tightened, and punch him square in the face, breaking his nose. A low crack follows the blow, and the Irishman grunts and curses, spitting blood.

Hyped up by the excitement of returning home, I punch him three more times in the face, enjoying every moment.

"What business does Boston have with the cartel?" my brother Andrei asks him again, calm and unmoved by my actions.

"You'll all be dead soon," he scowls at Andrei.

He's wasting our time. Deciding I'm not done having fun yet, I connect my fist with his face once more, beating the shit out of him—one punch after the other, his bright, fresh blood flying in the air. The Irishman is almost dead as he moans from the pain of each blow. My knuckles are aching only slightly, but it's nothing compared to the redness in his eyes or the swelling that burgeons on the side of his face. His lips are cracked, and blood trickles down already. I lift my hand again, ready to land a more brutal punch, but the Brigadier's voice cuts in.

"Enough," Andrei orders me, his voice vibrating through the room.

"But he threatened you," I whine, gritting my teeth, ready to kill the man in front of me. Andrei is the leader of the family. Our lives depend on him. I don't take threats against him lightly.

Andrei cocks his head to his side, signaling me again to stop. He doesn't say another word. He doesn't need to.

A flick of my wrist signals the soldiers to take the Irishman to the basement, where they'll torture him for hours. When the soldiers are done with him, he'll get a bullet. I really don't care. Right now, I'm too amped from the rush.

When we were teenagers, Andrei and I used to visit various clubs after a night like this. We would drink, snort a line of coke, and get between the legs of a few blondes.

But those days are over. Andrei is married now and is expecting his first child with his wife, Cora. These days, he is more than excited to head home to her as she waits for him with dinner ready. Heading off wordlessly, with a steely stare as if warning me again to behave, he leaves me standing in my empty condominium.

The life I left back in New York three years ago was one I'd enjoyed. Now, I return, finding that nothing has remained the same. *Disappointing.*

Unlike Andrei's home next door, which is filled with comfort and happiness with Cora, my condo feels like a prison cell. The walls seem to close in, and silence echoes around me, reminding me of the place's sterile emptiness. The sense of isolation and instability make me realize that my old life here is no longer the one I want.

If I were still in Russia, I would enjoy a bottle of vodka and a lovely group of young women. After a few hours, I would have my driver drop them off somewhere, rendering me alone again but completely satisfied, unlike now. Relationships are complicated. I'm too busy for complications.

But I can't overcome the feeling that something is missing from my life. Andrei's eyes light up when he talks about Cora and the planned arrival of his child, his legacy. It's almost as though he's taken a glimpse into the future, finding himself pleased with what awaits.

When I stepped foot on U.S. soil, Andrei pulled me into his office and sternly scolded me, making it clear the things I had done in Russia would never be tolerated here. To put it kindly, no more parties with women, drugs, and bad decisions. This was his way of telling me it was time to get my life in order. He has big plans for me. I must be ready.

Thinking about all this gives me a headache. I need a drink, and my empty condo doesn't even have a stocked bar yet. So, it's time for some fresh air. It's close to midnight, but this is New York, and they don't call it 'the city that never sleeps' for nothing.

As for that earlier invitation to the Coalition's private club, where there are plenty of drinks and women, I will pass, not wanting to reunite with old flings. Instead, I know a quiet place to enjoy a drink around the corner.

In the bathroom, I wash the blood from my hands, then trade my black suit for black jeans and a shirt.

After making my way down fifty-six floors in the elevator, I step into the dark and quiet lobby, greeted by a few tenants who welcome me home. As I walk toward the bulletproof glass doors, the men securing the entrance nod in my direction, showing their respect for me and my position in the Coalition as a Savin brother.

The cool air hits my face as I step outside into the street. The city is beautiful this time of year; the temperature is pleasantly cool, with gentle winds brushing against my cheeks and making them feel cold. My men stand a few feet behind me, which I dislike. An entourage is meant for celebrities, not for someone like me. Besides, Andrei is the leader of our family, the one we need to protect.

I prefer to be alone.

Now that some anger has left me, I need time to think about my next move after all that my brother shared today. I order security to stay. Reluctant, they begrudgingly listen.

My destination is a run-down bar in a New York City alleyway. It's been here since I was a kid. My brothers and I used to come here late at night as teenagers to enjoy a glass of vodka and talk about what girl or girls we were sleeping with. Pleasant memories, as if a lifetime ago.

People mostly frequent it right after work hours when they want a stiff drink that won't cost half their paycheck.

On the outside, someone might wonder how a bar like this stays open in an upscale part of New York City. Like most businesses associated with the Coalition, it's just a front for other activities, the not-so-legal ones.

The place turns out to be nearly empty, so I grab a stool for myself at the end of the bar. No other patrons are sitting in this corner, and this seat gives a clear view of the front and back doors. A few customers are scattered around the tables, too busy drinking and talking to pay attention to who's walking in and out.

The bartender immediately notices me and pours me vodka at around one hundred dollars a glass. He keeps a few bottles set aside for when my brothers and I come in, knowing we will always take the same expensive vodka our father drank.

It's not hard to notice a Savin in New York. Our complexion is darker than most Russians, and our black hair, squared chin, and hazel eyes make all five of us look alike.

Sitting here alone, lost in thoughts, I think of my time in Russia. Angry upon first arriving there, my brother Nikolai and I soon slaughtered a dozen men who didn't take Andrei's orders seriously. The older generation of Mafia men are too set in their ways, thinking their time and age make them bosses. So, they undermined the Brigadier's authority.

Under his leadership, the Savin brothers run operations using a different set of rules. We may be young, but we are in charge now and intend to change the face of organized crime.

As for me, I've been making money for the Savin business since closing my first deal at sixteen, investing in natural resources. Ten years later, that same deal has made the Coalition over a billion dollars, not exactly small change. So, does it matter what my age is? No. I will not be disrespected by a bunch of men riding the coattails of our work. We have made an example of them. Because of it, the other families in the Coalition have learned to respect us brothers, not because of our family name, but because they know we have earned it.

Now, my brothers and I will embark on a new journey that will once again be questioned, and we'll have to make an example of anyone who tries to undermine us. But we're ready for it. More than ready. Eager for it.

Together, the five of us can take any enemy who dares try to break our bond.

But am I really ready for the responsibility Andrei has asked of me? All night, my mind has been struggling, meandering to this question. I must push away the demons because it doesn't matter. The deal is sealed. Andrei has chosen my fate. Now, I'm a game piece on a chess board, walking through the moves I need to make if I'm going to win.

If. I sigh, letting the flames from my drink heat up my body, the sharp taste lingering in my mouth like traces of smoke after an explosion.

My glass is decidedly half-empty—metaphorically and literally—when the door creaks open. I peek up from the bar and see her walk in, observing a shift in everything around me, a sudden halt at the very second my eyes pick her up. Standing in front of me is a beautiful young woman with the prettiest smile I have ever seen.

Chapter Three

DMITRI

It's hard not to stare at her. She peeks around the tables, surveying the bar as if trying to find someone overlooking my direction. Her frame stretches tall, looking everywhere, assessing everything.

After a few minutes, she settles a few bar stools away, facing resolutely forward as if not even interested in the man sitting just a few feet away. It is as if she doesn't even see me, and this irks me, but in an oddly pleasant way.

Interesting.

Running my finger over the edge of my glass, letting the liquid swirl, I keep my eyes fixed on her. She still doesn't turn to steal a glance at me. Most women would. It feels futile all of a sudden that my eyes keep wandering to her, expecting that my sight searing into her beauty will force her to turn to face me.

But she either lacks that astute awareness, or she ignores me on purpose, knowing how it makes me squirm and writhe inside, setting every nerve on edge. I cannot imagine the former and won't allow myself to imagine the latter.

Women come easily when you're a Savin in New York City and Russia. It hardly requires any work on my part. There's always the thrill that comes with a bit of a chase, though.

This woman stands out in a crowd, appearing beautiful but not needy or promiscuous. My take is that this woman doesn't give a shit whether men notice her or not.

She is simply herself, filling the place with her presence. She wears a short, not too tight brown dress that complements her gorgeous, tanned, slightly muscular thighs. Those thighs are fully visible when the dress rides up due to how she confidently perches on her barstool.

Her brown hair with highlights ends at the center of her back. Her thick hair makes me think I would love to pull it later, as I am already picturing it.

"What can I get you?" The bartender steps in front of her, throwing down a napkin, ready to take her drink order.

"Um, do you happen to have coffee?" she asks.

"No, not at midnight." But just like me, he finds himself gazing at her, at how gorgeous she is. "I can make a fresh pot if you want, though. It's not a big deal," he responds, clearly flirting, smiling.

Her face still doesn't express much, but her voice is soft and steady. "Thank you. I promise to make it worth your time."

My heart almost explodes. *Will she make it worth his time? What the fuck?*

"Just a cup of coffee tonight?" He leans into the counter to get closer to her, surely near enough to smell the floral scent of her perfume, which I can detect from here. He is where I want to be.

"No," she says, smiling wryly. "When it's ready, please add a tequila shot to it. Top-shelf."

He laughs and disappears to make a fresh pot of coffee as though admitting she's way out of his league. But at least he tried.

Interesting choice. I don't think I've ever seen a woman order coffee and tequila at midnight in a bar. This woman is different. My interest is aroused further by it.

She sits pretending to be on her phone, but she's observant, her eyes glancing around the bar, completely aware of her surroundings. Aware of who comes in and out of the front door as well.

I see her casually glance at me. *Finally!*

Now, stage one of my game needs to come into play. I appear as though I am not paying attention to her while always watching—realizing in the next moment that it's probably the same tactic she uses, and I fell prey to it.

I usually would not try for small talk, especially tonight. Not when I've come here to be alone, but I'll play. The rules seem different, and something a little different is what I need.

About to say something to the beautiful woman, something distracts me in the corner of my eye, seeing this young finance kid approach. He staggers, his shirt roughly untucked and his hair ruffled. He has the air of a spoiled brat who always gets what he wants. They're always the same, those finance college graduates, high on life and starstruck from the blinding gaze of a bright future made of money. But none of them could ever dream of touching the sums I'm working with.

His speech is slightly slurred, though he tries to be charming. "What's a pretty girl doing in a bar like this late at night?"

This motherfucker! I usually don't care when some drunk asshole hits on a woman in a bar, but in my mind, I already claimed her for the night.

"Minding my business," she responds, making me delirious with joy to note that her voice is flat, and she refrains from glancing at him.

The response almost makes me chuckle. *My beautiful lady doesn't seem to like this asshole's advances.*

The kid, too young and oblivious, persists anyway, slipping over to her side, edging closer to her. I smell the alcohol on him, and the arrogance emanates from his pores just as strong.

"Come on, you ain't got to be like that. How about I buy you a few drinks and keep you company?"

"How about you go home and leave me the fuck alone?" She doesn't snap, raise her voice, or even flinch. Her face remains blank as she keeps her eyes on her phone.

There's something about her that exudes confidence as if she's dealt with her fair share of assholes before. I'd be stung if I were in that kid's place. And I'd persist, too, which is why I'm not surprised when the kid keeps pushing.

He grabs a strand of her hair and twirls it with his fingers. "You sure? We can have some fun."

At this point, this douchebag is pissing me off. "You heard the woman. She said to leave her alone," I growl. I don't share, and I don't like guys touching what I want. Plus, his buffoonery is plain annoying and pathetic.

"Dude, I'm not talking to you," he replies with an arrogant grin.

The bartender stops serving customers, no doubt wondering if he should phone for backup. I shake my head no. I have this under control, and he sees that immediately.

The old me would have already put a bullet in this fucker's head, but things have changed. I can't go around killing regular folks for every little reason. I've got to be more thoughtful about my choices because now, everything I do will be scrutinized and affect the Savin legacy. Another dead idiot at a bar would just be a mess, and no one would take pleasure in cleaning it up. So, instead, I sit and continue to sip my drink, deciding to just tease him.

Casually, I pull up my shirt, showing him my gun tucked in the back of my pants. "The woman said she's minding her business. I suggest you move on and do the same."

The kid's eyes widen at the sight, and he raises his hands in defeat. Shrugging, he glances at her in disdain. "If you want her, you can have her. She isn't even that hot."

He gives up his quest, still with his hands up, as he walks back to the table to join his friends and drink his beer, no doubt hoping to still have their respect. Laughter erupts from their table, and the kid buries his head in shame. I don't think his friends even know a gun was involved. Or, even deadlier, a Savin brother.

She looks in my direction, unimpressed. It's not the first time she's seen a gun. I'm no knight in shining armor. At least, she doesn't think so. Once again, she confirms she's not the kind of woman that usually catches my attention. Something tells me, she's been around violence.

I hold my glass up, angling my pretty drink to sparkle against the light. "Kind of late for coffee."

"I just got off work and still have things to do."

"Working late on a Friday night. Something tells me you work too much." There's an understandable tone behind my words.

"Yes, you can say that." Her response is flat again, hidden behind her otherwise emotional face. She sips her coffee again, slowly studying me, her eyes widening as she stares for a minute or two. Watching her bite on her bottom lip, I only hope she likes what she sees.

There's something about her sultry lips that makes me notice them. I bet they taste sweet. Too bad I won't know. Anyhow, I don't kiss women. Once you kiss them, they start to feel a romantic connection, asking for more than the one night I'm willing to give.

These past years, my priority has been making money for our family and proving to Andrei I'm ready for more responsibilities. Although I've enjoyed many women in Russia, I have always been honest with them about their expectations. I won't give them anything more than dinner and a nightcap. It might sound mean, but being truthful is the lesser evil than lying to them.

It's not that I don't believe in relationships. I've always envied Andrei and his marriage to Cora. He's loved that girl since they were both five. That's real love; I guess you can call them soulmates. But I've never found that person, and lately, I've started to doubt it will ever happen.

It still doesn't stop the allure of my straying thoughts. For once, I imagine how it would be to have her up against the wall, to crash my lips into hers, to push my cock in her.

I shake my head, hoping she didn't notice me staring back. "What do you do for work, Ms. Coffee and Tequila?"

"I'm the Chief Operating Officer of a few businesses. And you, do you work?" she asks with amusement. The title of Chief Operating Officer has me both impressed and undermined. So, she is one of those coldhearted, powerful women. The ones a man can't break.

I take a sip of my vodka, and after what seems like too long, I hear my own voice saying, "I help run the family business. Just got back from a long business trip."

Her eyebrows furrow at the uninspired response, "Well, I hope it was successful."

"Very." There's a short pause, and we use that time to sip our drinks.

My eyes remain on her. She holds my gaze with boldness now, entering into a battle of wits. No doubt she will win, and not because I give in and allow her to. More likely because her gaze is burning through me, making me oddly twitchy—and not only inside my pants.

"You're pretty young to run a few businesses."

"I work twenty hours a day. It was earned," she bites back as though demanding respect.

She's interesting, and yet again, I find myself turned on by her wit and intellect, raising my glass to her. "I have no doubt about that."

Speaking Russian, I tell the bartender, "Put her drink on my tab."

He nods in acknowledgment while I continue to sit, finishing my glass and watching her. She becomes nervous. Showing emotions for the first time, she drums her fingers against the bar.

"I'll take the bill." She catches the bartender's attention as though she suddenly must leave.

"Your drink is covered. Nothing to pay," he tells her, his eyes darting at me.

"Thank you," she responds back with an eye roll. She stands up, throws a hundred-dollar bill on the bar, and heads to the front door.

I want to say something to her, to tell her to stay, but I don't.

"Bathroom?" she asks, turning back to look at the bartender.

"Down that hall," he replies without looking up from the counter. She heads that way, disappearing, never glancing back.

It's probably time for me to leave as well. Andrei is bound to be keeping a watch. I throw a couple hundred-dollar bills on the bar and walk toward the exit door.

I don't want the night to end like this. I don't want the beautiful woman I've only just met to disappear and become someone to think about later while stroking my cock, alone. Walking past the door and down the hallway, my footsteps hurriedly take me to where she is.

Chapter Four

ELISE

I look at myself in the mirror. The late nights putting the deal together have started to take a toll on me, I notice, dabbing more concealer under both eyes, attempting to cover up the dark circles. Grabbing a paper towel, I splash water on it, dabbing my face and neck.

Calm down and get your shit together. Why did I come here tonight?

And who orders coffee at midnight? Okay, I do. Still, I should have ordered one of those silly New York drinks like a Manhattan or some shit with fruit in, letting me remain discreet. Then again, I hate doing things considered normal. No, I prefer standing out and getting noticed for being bold enough, for being different.

I give myself another look in the mirror, desperate to still be attractive at this hour. The knock on the door makes me jump. "I'll be right out!" Before I finish, another knock comes, followed by a click on the handle as the door slowly opens.

"Just finishing up," I say, but the words halt instantly, rolling down my throat. Standing in the open doorway is Dmitri.

Surprised, I stand still, staring at him, thinking how the many pictures I've seen have done him no justice. My mind starts wandering off, going places it shouldn't. How would it feel to run my fingers through his perfect black hair? His squared chin brings attention to the smirk he's displaying right now, as though he knows he's making my body warm.

He is definitely the most attractive man I have ever laid my eyes on. And that's a high bar. I work with a set of professionals with no morals. In return, the devil gives them all devilishly handsome looks to go with their wicked deeds.

Right now, in front of me, he's wearing a tight black shirt that displays his strained muscles against the fabric, a large tattoo creeping down his shoulder right above his right elbow. I would love to see where it starts. My thoughts stray, pulling with them vivid images, wild and erotic.

My body starts reacting to the beast of a man standing before me, tingles rushing through me, creeping from the tip of my fingers and spreading outward everywhere.

My heartbeat quickens, the walls around me seeming to spin. I try to keep myself steady, to not be overwhelmed by his eyes, too aware of the dampness forming between my thighs. I press them together to stop the ache of wanting him, my clit alight against my will.

Taking a step closer to me, he closes the door. "Never caught your name," he says.

Letting a few seconds burn through, I reply, "Elise."

He smirks and moves his lips slowly. "Beautiful." He takes another step closer.

"Thank you. I'm leaving." After quickly gathering my things, I turn to find him blocking the door as if to indicate there's no chance of me going anywhere.

Stepping back, I face the mirror to avoid eye contact and hide my fear. Does he know who I am?

He closes the distance between us until his body presses flush against mine, now so close that I can feel the bulge coming from his pants against my ass. His swelling is impressive, and my desire for him is just as thick.

In the mirror, his face stares back at me, his finger touching a strand of my hair, followed by a light touch on my left hip.

I bite my lower lip, swiftly developing an appetite to taste him, to have his lips on mine.

My breathing is hollowed, coming in quick bursts. I shudder when he touches me, sparking pleasures not felt in a long time. Goosebumps run down my neck and arms, my nipples simultaneously hardening to the point they are peeking through my dress and bra.

"Shit!" I curse under my breath.

His eyes glow, and the smile on his face extends into a knowing grin.

With my face flushed red, my body betrays me, the enemy's hands continuing to touch me lightly. I slightly turn my head downwards, hiding my eyes as he stares as if fixated.

He gently places his hand on my chin, turning my face to his until his lips claim mine.

Each thump of my heart aches against my ribs, but everything else seems frozen and silent, all my surroundings becoming blurry while he stays in focus. I'm spellbound, chained by desires suppressed for far too long. All I want is Dmitri.

Anything he wants from me, I will give.

My body is suddenly flooded with desires and cravings, flames licking through my skin. Nothing else matters now, just the burning intensity begging to be extinguished.

He moves away from my lips to tenderly—unexpectedly—kiss and nuzzle at the back of my neck just as his hands work to the front of my body. With both hands, he unties my dress, and it drops to the floor to leave me standing there, exposed in my bra and panties.

I brace myself for his touch. His hands make their way to my breasts as he squeezes them, moving my bra to the side so he can flick my already hardened nipples. His fingertips are not gentle—they're cut up and bruised as if he's just beaten someone.

And I don't mind it, finding it exhilarating.

Taking his index finger, he lightly touches it in just the right spot over my panties, which, now, are soaked. "That's what I thought." His voice is deep, sending chills rushing through me to hear his desire for me.

He pushes the lace to the side while his finger circles my clit, his other hand reaching to rub my ass, and he pauses to admire it. I swear I see him smile as though enjoying what he sees. My pussy gushes in response. "Blayd," he mutters.

He slowly inserts his finger into my pussy, moving in and out. One finger becomes two, then three, gliding in and out easily with my wetness. Feeling his forcefulness, I spread my legs farther and softly moan. My mind is telling me I should stop this, that I've come here tonight on a recon mission, not to scream Dmitri's name in the bar's bathroom.

But when I open my mouth, the only thing that comes out is, "Oh God, yes!"

I've just invited him to violate me, to own my body.

Suddenly, he stops touching me, leaving me still and unable to move, powerless. He's pinned me between his hard body and the bathroom counter. I eye him, waiting for his next move, biting my lower lip and holding my breath at the thought of never feeling his hands on me again.

Then, as two fingers move to each side of my waist, he tugs my panties, slithering them down my thighs until they hit the floor. When I hear his zipper come down, I submit to my desires and let him take control, legs widening again, pussy beyond wet.

His hand touches the lowest part of my back as he leans me forward, bending me over, leaning my ass into his cock. His other hand spreads my ass cheeks open, then gently reaches around the front to softly stroke the nub of my dancing clit, making my juices dribble out.

Without any warning, his cock tip also dances for a second at my opening, stroking it briefly before pushing deep into me, thrusting inside, creating the sound of wetness and pleasure.

Placing my hands on both sides of the mirror, holding myself up, he continues to thrust his big cock deep into me, only now and then reaching down again to run a titillating fingertip over my clitoris. He edges back its skin, stroking millimeter by millimeter on my little engorged nub, making me shudder, and making me moan, "Fuck me." My wetness grows, and my legs are clamping his cock inside me, crossing over to increase the pressure on my magic spot.

The sounds coming from my mouth only make him fuck me harder, forcing him deeper into me. He's enjoying how I've now closed my legs, making this feel even more illicit as if he is taking me without asking.

He's watching me in the mirror, his mouth open, grunting, eyes glazed.

Shyly, I turn my head when he says, "Look at me. I need to see you come on my cock." I do as he commands. We both continue to experience this high with our eyes locked on one another. He's amused at the fact that I am losing control. My eyes are half closed, and I feel every inch of him.

His hand comes around my waist again, now using two fingers to trap my clitoris, rolling it between them. With every thrust, he circles his fingers around my clit until I can no longer maintain composure, letting free a scream, my body quivering as I shatter on his cock, sending him into a frenzy. "That's my good girl."

There is nothing romantic about this moment, no lovemaking happening here. This is purely the most amazing fuck I've ever had in my lifetime, the rawness of our moment sending shockwaves exploding through me.

I may never experience this again.

My body arches into his when I come. It doesn't take much longer before he glides his cock in and out of me harder, making sure every inch is palpable. "You feel so good, baby," he whispers in my ear as he tangles my hair in his fingers, pulling my head back.

A sensation builds up in me. His hand smacks my ass, and I scream and explode again, my pussy tightening around his cock in a frenzy.

He erupts inside me as I'm still panting and coming down from my high, now feeling the mixture of his sweat and liquids inside of me, running like a delicious cascade down my thighs.

We both stand there for a moment, my eyes unable to meet him because of the guilt of knowing that what we just did should not have happened.

He slowly pulls out of me and zips up his pants as if we did nothing at all while leaving me dripping from him, filled with his salty, delicious cum.

What have I done?

I'm known not to lose control, always calm and sensible. Something about him has made me behave like this, getting me caught up in the moment. Deciding what to do next, I stand still, half-naked and sweaty, coming down from the best orgasm ever, my chest rising rapidly. In the aftermath, my fingers urgently want to slide back between my legs to my clit, to extract every shudder from it, to make it jitter again, but I fight against this secret urge.

Dmitri starts to walk out of the bathroom, and I feel embarrassed by the reality of what just happened.

Before he opens the door, he pauses. Turning around, he walks back to me and kisses me on the cheek. "I'll see you later, baby." My heart speeds up at the sentiment.

And, like that, the devil I have just let fuck me in the bar bathroom disappears.

Fuck me! I fucked up!

Chapter Five

ELISE

A loud sound stirs me awake. *What the hell?*

Squinting, I look at my phone. *Dammit!*

Quickly, my body jumps from the bed, hurtling to the window to see the green garbage truck driving through the alleyway, clattering and clanging as it goes, picking up the week's trash.

Did I really forget to set my alarm clock? Shit!

Then, everything from the night before piles back into my consciousness. I left the bar feeling ashamed, excited, satisfied, and slightly sore. A chaotic mash of emotions has left me exhausted and confused—excited one moment, a guilty mess the next.

Tossing and turning, unable to sleep, I recall replaying what happened in the bathroom, fighting the urge to run my fingers under the sheets. I usually don't sleep much, but restless dreams of Dmitri made keeping my eyes closed even harder.

After a quick shower and throwing on a dress, I brush my hair into a high pony and run outside. Alejandro is already out there, waiting with the SUV to take me to work.

He stares at me through the rearview mirror as I put on my make-up. I never run late for work, unready and flustered. The way I feel right now is certainly not something to get used to and mustn't happen again. No, Dmitri won't happen again. I shove thoughts of him down into the farthest parts of my mind, hoping they don't crawl back up.

"You're late," Jessica says, seeing me walk up the stairs and head down the hall to my office.

"It's eight o'clock." Already panicky, I'm now annoyed at the statement.

"Yeah, but you're usually here before seven and before anyone else gets here."

I grit my teeth and exhale slowly, holding back the urge to yell. "I worked late. Didn't sleep well either."

She knows I haven't slept through the night ever since joining the cartel. The hasty clicking of her shoes on the floor almost matches mine. We are practically on autopilot at this point.

"There's a situation in there before you walk in," Jessica informs me, pointing her finger to my office down the hall.

"Like what?" I'm still annoyed and need time to gather my thoughts, wondering why she hasn't even brought me coffee.

"Well, Liam says you should take care of it. He and Carlos aren't coming in until later."

Assholes! I walk into the office at eight o'clock, and apparently, they think I'm late, but the guys wander in whenever they want, depending on how many women and how much blow they've had the night before. Worse still, no one seems to care.

Liam is known for being a heartbreaker and isn't planning to settle anytime soon. He's handsome, rich, and exhibits money as if it's a tattoo. Plus, he has an endless supply of cocaine that the women love to snort in exchange for sex and blowjobs. His cousin Carlos is Liam's right hand, overseeing business and getting into trouble.

I, of course, stand to his left, helping run a multi-billion-dollar cartel operation, mainly importing coke with Liam and Carlos. Yet I don't even know how it feels to be high. Though I work for the cartel, I don't do drugs. *Isn't that ironic?* While most people love coke, I just love money.

There is no such thing as equity in the cartel. It's all about rank. Unless you're a woman, in which case, your position doesn't matter at all. My entire existence in the cartel is to close the financial statements, wash the money, and run the tequila bars.

"Well, what or who is in my office?" My mood moves from annoyed to angry as Jessica has a habit of not getting to the point. The snap startles her.

"Diego has Mr. Banks in there. Something about permits not getting approved."

Great way to start my morning. "Where is my coffee?"

Startled by my bark, Jessica turns, heading to the kitchen. She's efficient and dependable, so I should take it easy with her. But not today. Today, I'm irritated, and everyone's fair game.

During the entire ride into the office and my conversation with Jessica, only a single thought has pervaded, that of Dmitri standing behind me, his lips on mine, his cock deep in me. An office visit from Mr. Banks is precisely what I need now. A distraction from last night.

I head straight for my desk, never making eye contact with Mr. Banks or the cartel men. Though fully aware of Mr. Banks sitting on the opposite side of my desk, I let him sweat for a bit. Standing in front of my chair, I read emails, making him wait for me to speak. My quietness is causing him some uneasiness, but that's fully intended.

He squirms slightly, clothes ruffling, and the chair squeaks. I still don't pay him any attention. *Let him sweat.*

"Coffee, Elise." Jessica strides in, trying not to notice Mr. Banks either. He must be feeling invisible by now.

"Thank you, Jessica." She places the cup on my desk and quietly sneaks out as I continue to work. After a silent five minutes, I sit in my chair and acknowledge Mr. Banks, who now has beads of sweat on his forehead and temples and an underarm stain spreading.

"Mr. Banks, our permits have not been approved yet." I sip my coffee, staring.

He looks around at the three cartel men standing around the office, then at me. He starts to stutter, "Well, there's a lot of things to work through, and it's taking more time than I anticipated."

My voice stays level and calm, my eyes fixed on him. "Mr. Banks, that college tuition we are paying for your daughter is supposed to assure us that you will fix any 'things' that come up, right?"

Patiently sipping my coffee, I wait for Mr. Banks to produce some bullshit reason why my permits are still sitting on his desk without approval.

"Yes, but—"

He's about to give me a bunch of excuses I don't care about, so I cut him off. "Mr. Banks, is your wife headed to her job as a nurse at the Medical Center right now? She starts at nine o'clock, so she should be on her way, right?"

"Yes. Why?" he answers, eyes widening, scared. The fear in the air is palpable, thick, cold. But this isn't his first time working with the cartel, so he should know where this is headed.

"Diego, please do me the favor of collecting Mrs. Banks when she arrives at work and bring her to me. Also, stop by the supply store and pick up a big box to send her head to their daughter."

I turn to my computer and start typing, ignoring everyone around me.

The weight of my words shakes the room for a second, hearing a startled gasp escape the lips of the frightened man before me.

"Yes, Elise," Diego quickly replies.

"Wait!" Mr. Banks calls out. His voice shakes, almost rivaling the trembling of his hands. Damp marks start to show even worse on his shirt, and the beads of sweat on his fleshy face are running now. "I'll take care of it."

"By the end of the day, Mr. Banks?"

"Yes." Mr. Banks is looking at me, eyes wide open, hands in the air, begging for a second chance. I'm in no mood to kill him today, plus I do really need those permits.

"Diego, please escort Mr. Banks out of my office and make sure he gets my permits approved by the end of the day. If he fails to do so, shoot him in the head and bring his wife to me."

I go back to typing.

"Yes, Elise." Diego grabs Mr. Banks' arm and escorts him out of my office and the building. And it's true. If the permits aren't approved today, I won't think twice about killing them. And I'll have Diego keep killing whoever is necessary until my permits come through.

I've spent the last three months working on this deal, and those permits are essential to moving forward. At the age of twenty-five, I'm brokering an agreement between the cartel, Bratva, and Italian Mob to share and each own part of the ports needed to import goods for all our various illegal businesses.

In the last three years, these three groups of men have killed hundreds of each other's soldiers and management, resulting in profit losses for everyone. Money is one thing these businessmen love more than anything else, even more than they love women.

I've spent hundreds of hours generating reports on all the business losses each group has suffered because of their inability to negotiate and work together.

After three months of sitting with each team, negotiating, and working out numbers to benefit all parties, I finally have all three bosses willing to approve the deal—Liam, the Brigadier, and Mr. Bianchi. So, I won't let some government asshole stall it because of his inability to approve some lousy permits. That's also why I need to know why Dmitri's in town.

His brother, the Brigadier, is one-third of my deal.

Andrei does not negotiate with others, especially the cartel, so I was surprised when he agreed to the deal. After months of collaboration with him, he ultimately supports this deal and plans to proceed with closing.

So why, after three years, did Dmitri show up to help his brother run the family business without notice? Why, when we are so close to closing this?

I take a moment and enjoy the quietness in my office after this shitty morning, taking a sip of my coffee, sitting back in my chair, and letting my mind return to last night to Dmitri.

"Mr. Banks?" Liam asks as he walks in with a bottle of water, attempting to sober up.

I sit up immediately, hoping he didn't catch me daydreaming. "I'm taking care of it."

"You always do." He sits in the chair across from my desk.

"Good night?" I ask.

"Always." He starts to laugh and takes a drink. The water always indicates that he's hungover, so I must compensate for his lack of work today.

"You find out anything about Dmitri?" he asks, wiping a few drops of water off his chin and frowning when some liquid trickles onto his pants.

"I'm working on it." I look away so my eyes can't tell him about my lies. Sometimes, he knows me too well and can see when I'm not entirely truthful.

"Good girl." A smile forms on his face, his eyes almost sleepy. "What would I do without you?"

"Nothing, apparently," I say softly, and he winks.

He heads to the door but pauses for a moment. "Did you have a fun night in the city?"

What, why? Does he know about last night already?

"Just a recon mission." Turning to my computer, I start typing again, deflecting nervousness.

He stays quiet for a moment, almost forgetting his train of thought. Before he exits, he turns to me. "I need you to attend the mayor's fundraiser on Tuesday. I'll be visiting Houston for a meeting with my father and brothers."

Señor Martinez is head of the Martinez Cartel. He doesn't come to the States often because he's wanted by every law enforcement agency. Liam runs the U.S. for the cartel. If he's coming over the border, something big is happening. Now, I'm interested in what this meeting could be about.

"Houston ... Anything I need to know?" This is the first time I've heard about this trip.

"I'll keep you updated when I return. Take care of everything while Carlos and I are away."

"I always do." It's an honest answer because around here, I do everything.

He takes a sip of water, winks again, and walks out, leaving me to sip on my coffee and contemplate that something about Houston just doesn't sit right.

Chapter Six

ELISE

Liam has been my boss for a long time, and he knows I'll never say no to him, no matter what he asks of me. When I first came to New York, I was eighteen and didn't know anyone. It was a new world in a more prominent place than anywhere I'd ever been. It was too easy to get swallowed up by everything—the fear, uncertainties, and weight of everyday life.

A student at one of the city's most prestigious universities on scholarships and taking out massive student loans, I had little money saved and needed a job. Working as a bartender at a tequila bar sounded appealing because the tips were too good to pass up, averaging around two hundred dollars a shift.

I have always been a hard worker. Liam immediately noticed me, moving me up to shift manager after two months. I relished every challenge and pushed myself further, becoming the bar manager after six months.

Before completing my first year at college, I was already managing all his tequila bars in New York, and by the end of my second college year, all cartel-owned tequila bars in New York and New Jersey were under my management. By the time I entered the master's program at twenty-two, Liam had appointed me Chief Operating Officer of the entire Martinez Tequila Bar Corporation. You could say it had been a fast-track promotion.

At first, it seemed strange, his motives in question. I was young and attractive with big breasts and a nice round ass, thanks to daily workouts. I assumed he just wanted to get between my legs. It was more than pos-sible. Women get promoted all the time because they sleep with pivotal men.

However, he never made a pass, never said lewd things, or told me my ass looked good in a certain tight black skirt—none of that. Instead, he had all the men pay close attention to me, watch me, and escort me to the train station at night on my way home, keeping me safe, all things these men didn't do for any other employees. It felt like a privilege, although I'd tell myself I'd earned it, becoming an asset he couldn't afford to lose.

He would occasionally hang out at the bar when I worked, having a drink or busy doing work, as though trying to be close to me. There was a certain pleasure in having him around, and I started to have a crush on him, liking how he made me feel special. At one point, I even thought I loved him. The guys in New York were aggressive, but Liam ... Well, he was a mystery. He never made any advances toward me, and in time, we established a real friendship.

When he appointed me as his third-in-command, I stopped myself from falling deeper in love with him. Now, the thought makes me chuck-le, realizing I didn't love him. I only thought so because a guy had never paid that much attention to me before or made me feel so special.

Deciding the opportunity was more important than a guy who gave me butterflies, I dove straight into my work. He even stopped flirting with me after appointing me to my new role. Our relationship is strictly family when he's not barking orders at me.

There were always rumors that the bars were a front for the cartel. They carried a lot of security, particularly men with guns, hanging around and conducting business meetings in the various back rooms. There was always an air of secrecy around them, hushed whispers and shifty glances while they downed hard liquor and smoked cigars.

You could tell these men were relaxed and unbothered by the authorities, that they were in a safe place. I was wise to know that it had something to do with illegal activities.

Honestly, I didn't care. I was far too busy making great money, getting promoted, and becoming a boss in my own right. Then came the one day that changed my life so vividly.

***

A few years ago, I worked late one night on financial statements, trying to wash some extra cash. Usually, Liam or Carlos would tell me to go home, but that night, they didn't.

It was a weeknight, so the bar closed early.

It was quiet, then came the sound of men arguing in Liam's office. The voices bounced against the walls, rising and falling, spliced with yells and grave threats. The sounds were muffled from where I was, so I walked closer to find Liam's office door closed.

The whimpering voice became clear. "Mr. Martinez, I swear I didn't steal your money. I don't know what happened to it."

"I don't like liars." That was Liam on the other side. He sounded different. There was a soft growl to his words and a lingering deadliness. I took a deep breath, narrowed my eyes, and tried to determine what was happening.

"No! No!" the whimpering man's desperate voice shot out. Suddenly, a crack of a gunshot ricocheted through the air. I cupped my mouth and held my breath, holding back a gasp. The gunshot was followed by the unmistakable thump of a body hitting the floor.

My heart raced, thudding painfully against my chest. So many thoughts rushed through my mind, scrambling to be heard. "Run! Run!" the voices in my head echoed frantically. Yet my legs were still and numb, my hands trembled, and my ears rang from that gunshot. Before I could decide what to do next, his office door flung open. Liam stood before me.

Sweat broke out from my forehead, and I gulped. My lips quivered as I looked up at him. "You weren't supposed to be here, Elise." There was crimson on his formerly flawless white button-down shirt. His rolled-up sleeves made it easy to see several busted knuckles.

I found my voice and kept it steady, easing my breath, pushing aside whatever fear washed through my body. It was as if another part of my brain had been unlocked, one at ease with this brutality and the deadly vibe still ringing in the air.

"I was working late. I'm here. Do you need my assistance?" My eyes peered past his feet to the body on the floor. Liam was still staring at me, waiting to see how I would respond to the hideous sight. So, I didn't. Instead, I looked at him, expressionless, awaiting his response.

"Since you're here, call the cleaners and have them take care of my office."

"I'll take care of it." Moving past him, past the dead body and the men watching me, I picked up the phone. A slight shiver ran up my spine. I clenched the phone, channeling those short bursts of anxiety into my tight grip.

Liam and the men disappeared quickly as I called the number Carlos handed to me. I casually waited for the cleaners to arrive, to clear the body, and clean the blood off the floor.

I went home scared, not knowing if a man with a gun would be waiting when I opened my door. I didn't sleep much that night and came into the office early the following day.

Carlos was waiting for me there. They were usually not in the office before me, so something was up.

"I have some business at the ports today. Liam thinks it's time to expand some of your responsibilities." Carlos stood near my door, blocking me if I wanted to run out.

"Absolutely!" I grabbed my coffee and followed him out the door.

When we arrived at the port, no business was waiting for me.

Instead, I found a Russian man tied to a chair, bloody and begging for his life. The ropes dug into the man's skin, and his face was swollen and bruised. His head wobbled from side to side, and his breathing was labored. His wrists had deep purple bruises and burn marks, and his fingers were lacerated.

Carlos only laughed, finding it amusing that the man was begging for his life.

He watched me closely, his dark eyes penetrating deeply. He was checking for flinches and hesitation, deciding whether I could be trusted. Or he just wanted to read every emotion on my face to find out what I was thinking. I tried to give little away.

"Elise, we need the name of the man who ordered the hit yesterday. Please have Ivanov tell you who ordered it." Carlos stepped back and walked toward the side of the room where the other cartel men were standing.

I focused on Mr. Ivanov. It was just him and me. What should I do next? I glanced over at Carlos to see him watching me. Liam and Carlos were testing me, and I realized that in that second.

"Mr. Ivanov, who ordered the hit?" I stood before the man tied to a metal chair.

He laughed at me. "Silly girl, I'm not saying shit to you."

I'd assumed wrongly about him, thinking he'd say anything to have them spare his life, but there he was, already condescending at the first chance he got.

I scanned around the room. The man beside Carlos, someone I knew, was Diego, one of Liam's top soldiers. He and a few more cartel men were watching, waiting to see me fail.

A hammer was on the floor, so I strode to pick it up.

My nerves were shaky, but I tried to steady myself and focus on the task. Besides that, it was easy to get fueled by that man's condescending look and the way he had called me a silly girl. Sure, I was scared, but I'd be in that same chair next if I didn't do what Carlos expected.

I calmed myself and steadily asked, "Mr. Ivanov, who ordered the hit?"

He paused for a moment, looking me over, no doubt thinking I couldn't do it. A brief glint came to his eyes, then his lips began to stretch into a malicious grin. Before he could laugh at me again, I struck him hard on his kneecap with the hammer with all my strength.

Mr. Ivanov underestimated me. This wasn't my first time hitting a man.

When I was thirteen, I found my mother getting beaten by a boyfriend. When my sister tried to stop him, he slapped her and threw her across the room. I had also seen men in the trailer park beat people up before, so violence wasn't new. Grabbing a bat nearby, I hit her boyfriend across his skull, causing him to be hospitalized. Making sure he didn't press charges, I threatened to turn over his drugs to the cops. So, he lied and reported a robber had done it.

He never saw my mother or us again after that.

"Fucking bitch!" the captive screamed. The chair creaked when he wobbled, vibrating from the pain.

I stood before him. He was no longer laughing. "Mr. Ivanov, who ordered the hit?"

"Fuck you!" So, I hit his other kneecap. It snapped like a cracker. More screams.

I stepped back to stand in front of him again, maintaining a calm demeanor because I had an audience. With each second that passed, I found myself getting bolder.

"Mr. Ivanov, who ordered the hit?"

"Fuck you." I hit him again.

"I can keep this up all day, Mr. Ivanov. Who ordered the hit?" I raised the hammer high, and he flinched, his face pale and covered in sweat.

"I don't know," he yelled, the veins on his neck strained. Saliva dribbled down the side of his mouth, and his head fell forward, his breathing becoming more difficult.

I smiled and started hitting him on the head with the hammer, copious blood flowing from his scalp down his face, filling both eyes.

"Mr. Ivanov, who ordered the hit?"

"I don't know." More hits to his head. His eyes were dull as he managed to raise his head to look at me. I lifted my hand again, ready to strike, a rush inside me, a surge of adrenaline shooting through my veins. My grip on the weapon was tighter than before, and my eyes narrowed on his head, ready to deal even more damage.

Just before I was ready to strike again, he yelled, "Stop! Stop! Orlov! Orlov ordered the hit."

Cleared of the need to hit him again, I said, "Thank you, Mr. Ivanov. Now, was that so hard? You could have saved us a lot of time and energy if you had just said that from the beginning."

I slightly paused, considering what I'd just done. My head turned to Carlos, and he nodded, and it was clear what he expected me to do next. Walking over to Diego, I handed him the hammer and grabbed the gun from his hand to point it at Mr. Ivanov. I swallowed hard. My hand was unsteady, so I had to use both of them. I felt like stopping, dropping the gun, and breaking for it. But that would be a death sentence, and I'd already come this far.

My hands trembled, leveling the gun at Mr. Ivanov. Steady.

I took a deep breath, closed my eyes, and pulled the trigger. The resistance against my pull knocked back my finger, but I squeezed harder, the sound deafening and the stench of smoke nauseating. My eyes opened again slowly, just in time to see Mr. Ivanov arching back, blood spewing from his mouth, also from his nostrils and even his ears.

I pulled that trigger two more times to make sure he was dead.

***

That day, with a hammer and a gun, I became an official member of the Martinez Cartel. Nothing had prepared me for what Liam had planned for me.

Before I could realize it, the eighteen-year-old bartender had ceased to exist, and before Liam stood the woman he'd turned me into.

Now, I rule by fear, too. But fear is also what drives me because Liam will never let me go, never let me leave the cartel. I'm too much of an asset to him. He owns me.

This life would terrify most women. But I made my choice that day at the warehouse. It doesn't matter now if it was right because once you're in the cartel, the only way out is by death.

Chapter Seven

ANDREI SAVIN

Dmitri walks into my office. I watch him closely. His face sags a bit, dark circles nestling under both eyes.

"How was your first night back home, brother?" I ask him.

"It was good. I'm happy to be back in New York." He nonchalantly shrugs.

"You look tired. Not sleeping well?"

I invite him to sit by me. He's only been home for twenty-four hours, and it already looks like something's on his mind.

"Time difference," he responds, moving to the seat next to me on my office couch, avoiding eye contact.

As much as I'm sure the seven-hour time difference is affecting him, I'm pretty sure the bar he headed to late last night is also to blame. I trust my brother, but he's been in Russia for three years, so keeping an eye on him is necessary right now. He's family, and that's important, but I must make sure he stays in line.

Our father died ten years ago. His car was parked at a red light when another rolled by and rained a hail of bullets into it. The Brigadier and his soldiers that day were presumed dead on the spot. He never had a chance, but at least the men who shot him died three days later.

I am the oldest Savin brother. His seat as Brigadier was passed to me. I was bestowed the title when I was only twenty and still in college. My brother Dmitri is only two years younger, so we were close growing up. We were always brothers and friends, the best of both. The two of us learned much from our father about the family businesses and the Coalition.

This would be our legacy one day.

I changed the day I became Brigadier, having no choice in that. The college kid in me had ceased to exist. I was now head of the Savin family, with a mother, four brothers, and a future wife to provide for. My priority shifted to running the family's businesses in New York and solidifying my place as a Bratva leader.

Dmitri wanted to be my second-in-command and run the businesses by my side. Though just eighteen at the time, he'd always been a brilliant kid, and the business side of the Savin family came easily to him. I'd always tease him about his gift for numbers and his tight scrutiny of how the business worked. Dmitri always had an idea in his head, even helping close a billion-dollar deal in natural resources while still in high school.

But he was selfish. Sometimes, I wish he'd take a step back and think things through before making decisions, never thinking beyond himself or accepting responsibility for anything.

Dmitri resorted to violence before asking questions, also spending too much time chasing women. Self-control makes a good Brigadier, not violence and hasty decision-making.

I sent him to college because he wasn't ready for a leadership role. That decision strained our relationship. He saw it as spite against his character, not as something done in his best interest.

"It's what Father would have wanted," I tried to reason, but he brushed that aside and held on to his rage. He took my decision as a lack of faith in him, and in a way, it pushed him to try and prove himself worthy. After receiving a college degree in business, he proved he could be a vital leader for our family. As a reward, I put him in charge of our Russian companies.

Without our father's dictatorship, and because my brothers and I were so young, our men in Russia weren't running the businesses in accordance with my or Dmitri's orders. It was time for the Savin brothers to step foot in Russia permanently.

With the help of our brother, Nikolai, now serving as the Colonel of the Coalition's Army, Dmitri was able to get the men in Russia to fall in line. If they didn't, they were replaced. We proved the Savin brothers were in charge. Today, our Russian-based businesses and affairs operate successfully and completely under Dmitri's control. Or, more specifically, under my own. But recent family affairs have changed our priorities.

Now, I need him home with me in New York.

A few weeks ago, Pakhan, the leader of the Coalition, invited me to enjoy a cigar with him. He then asked the men to leave, expressing a need to speak with me privately.

Shifting in his seat, he secretly told me he had cancer.

Sick and on his deathbed, the doctors weren't giving him more than eighteen months. He and his wife had only daughters, so he would need to name the next Pakhan soon. Coughing but still prideful, he gazed into my face and said, "You will be the one."

That day changed everything. Being Pakhan is the highest honor my uncle could give me.

It also means I must pass the Brigadier seat to one of my brothers.

There are only five Brigadiers in the Coalition. Our family has held one of these positions for generations. The Savin family is Coalition legacy, so our uncle being the Pakhan furthered our high status in the Russian Bratva. The Savin brothers may be young, but we are the most feared in the underground world.

Dmitri is the second eldest Savin son, and the honor of being Brigadier belongs to him. Plus, Nikolai already holds a leadership spot as the Colonel and ruler of our army. Our youngest twin brothers, Anton and Alexi, serve as Coalition assassins.

Dmitri is ready for his new role.

During his time in Russia, he showed me his teenage boy antics were over. Sure, he and Nikolai had loads of fun in Russia with the ladies, but that was expected from young Bratva men. His work with our businesses shows me he can rule by my side.

So, I called Dmitri, telling him it was time for him to come home and be the new Brigadier. He accepted.

Besides Pakhan, my brothers, and I, no one else is privy to our current plan. Until his announcement, Pakhan's life and power are in jeopardy. Therefore, this news must remain a secret.

As the new Pakhan, I would like to save a few men's lives while making money. That's why I agreed to Elise's deal. Her plan can work for all of us.

Dmitri gets up and walks over to the bar in the corner of my office. He pours himself a drink and turns to me, offering a glass. I shake my head. We have serious business to talk about.

"The port deal is expected to close soon."

"The deal with the cartel and Mob?" Dmitri is still catching up on things in the U.S. I plan to close the deal before handing it off to him. It's best that way.

"Yes. I've vetted the plan. It will be good for us."

He frowns deeply, doubts forming in his eyes. "You sure? They've killed many of our men. We have been enemies with the cartel for a long time."

Dmitri is questioning my authority. I have to keep things clear and firm. "We have also killed many of their men. The cartel and Italians are still our enemies. This deal is specifically for importing goods."

"Dad would never deal with the cartel. He and Señor Martinez were the worst of enemies," he reminds me.

"But I'm making a deal with Liam, not his father. And, brother, don't ever question my decisions. Remember, I'm still the Brigadier. Just because we share the same blood, it doesn't mean I won't put you in the basement and remind you of that fact," I state with a clenched jaw.

His gaze becomes distant, and he apologizes. "I'm sorry, brother."

Even when he becomes the new Brigadier, I'll still be in charge as the Pakhan, ruler of the Coalition and the most powerful man in the Bratva world. He knows I will always outrank him. It's not only because it's my birthright but because it was also earned.

"We have a meeting in a week with the cartel woman. The permits should be approved and in place. We'll need to sign contracts for various businesses. All three bosses will be there. I want you to ensure I have backup at the meeting."

"Yes, Flemiche's. I've already told the snipers where to be." I see he's jumped straight into work mode since being home.

Then he adds, "This cartel woman, is she hot? Have you tasted what's between her legs yet?" He leans back in the chair, arms crossed behind his head. His lips spread into a taunting grin, and his eyes flicker. *What an asshole!*

When I first saw Elise, I immediately noticed what a beautiful woman she was. If it had been years earlier, before I'd married Cora, I might have thought about having more than just a regular meeting with her. But it's no secret I'm a one-woman kind of man these days. Even Dmitri knows I'm fully committed to my wife.

He's just being an asshole as payback for my scolding earlier.

Elise has proven herself indispensable for the cartel, and I've got future plans for her, so I can't have my brother's cock causing any complications. "She's off limits. Knowing her, you don't have a chance. But it might be fun watching you try. She's all about business."

"Challenge accepted." Dmitri gets up and walks out of my office, shaking his head and chuckling.

"Good luck," I call out.

***

When I got a call from a woman working for the cartel, I was surprised, having heard about her from our intel. Elise Walsh had worked her way up from bartender to cartel boss, quite an intriguing story, and not one you hear every day. So, when she wanted to meet, I was curious and agreed.

When the cartel's third-in-command walked into a bar full of Russians, she was either fearless or dumb. She sat on an empty bar stool, and people took notice. Whispers began, voices hushed, necks craned, eyes straining. She had the calm demeanor of a woman aware of where she was.

The bartender took her order and promptly set the coffee cup in front of her.

One of the men, a Coalition associate yet no more than an errand boy, had been watching her from the back of the room and, for some reason, decided to walk her way. I watched, waiting to see what was about to happen.

The associate got a few feet behind her before he growled and yelled at her loudly, "Cartel bitch, you're not welcome here. Get the fuck out, or my bullet will gladly help you exit."

The sudden outburst drew more attention, and people shifted in their seats, eager to join in. My eyes drifted back to her.

She smiled, never looking back at him. She didn't have to. She was watching him and anyone behind her through the mirrors behind the bar. She reached into her purse, pulling out something.

It made me straighten, still watching her. Maybe pepper spray? That would be hilarious. Something glimmered in her hand, and a collective gasp erupted.

A grenade! She held it gently in her left hand as though it was a delicate cupcake.

"If I go to hell tonight, I'm taking everyone in this bar with me. I suggest you go back to enjoying your drink." With her other hand, she continued to lift her coffee calmly.

Everyone in the bar kept watching, trying to decide if they should run or pray, all waiting to follow my lead. She had balls bigger than the man standing behind her, I thought with admiration. It was her sense of calm that really did it for me.

She'd definitely earned her spot in Liam's organization, and her demeanor proved that. I was now really interested in what she had to say.

After a few minutes of tense silence, this spectacle had gone on too long for my patience. I ordered the man to go back and enjoy his drink and leave her alone, saying all that in Russian so that she didn't know I was giving him an order.

He nodded and quietly walked back to his seat, acutely aware that I'd received his little show poorly. I couldn't blame the men for being angry and hating her. She was cartel. It didn't matter if she hadn't done anything personally to them.

We'd been at war with the cartel and Italians, fighting over ports and shipments for years. We had lost a lot of men, ones who used to drink in this very same bar. Indeed, she hadn't been expecting a smooth welcome.

"Thank you, Mr. Brigadier." She turned to me, easing her fingers on the grenade she placed back in her purse. She wasn't sweating or fidgeting. Maybe she hadn't been bluffing about using that grenade.

"I'm ready for our meeting when you are," she continued, smiling.

I wondered if she knew who I was while watching her. But then again, a woman like her would always do her homework before class. She knew who and where I was, probably from the moment she'd walked in.

"This way." I signaled to her, heading to the side door next to which I'd been standing. She cautiously got off her stool, placed a hundred bill on the bar, and walked my way.

"Well played," I whispered as we walked through the door.

"I didn't come to play, Brigadier. I came to talk business." Her tone was flat and business-like, leaving no wiggle room for anything else.

The back meeting room was small but served a purpose. I motioned for Elise to sit on one side of the table as I sat across from her. She must have been very aware of the two Russian men standing behind her. But if she was bothered by that, she didn't show it.

She went straight to business. "Brigadier, I have a proposal for you."

I waved my hand. "The cartel has nothing to offer me."

"How about you give me ten minutes? If you aren't interested, then I'll leave."

"Elise, I'll give you five." I sat back in my chair, ready to listen to what she was offering. She was curious, which was why I afforded her those five minutes.

"Brigadier, the Russian war with the cartel and Italians over the ports has cost you millions of dollars and many soldiers. It costs the cartel and Italians equally. So," she said, leaning closer as if conspiratorial, "I have a plan that can financially benefit all three families and end all the fighting over port space."

I stroked my chin but said nothing. She wasn't wrong about all that. I'd lost a lot of money due to our differences over the ports.

She reached into her purse and took out a tablet. My men dipped their hands into their jackets when she moved, eyes locked on her. I wasn't afraid of anything, and she didn't seem to care.

"Brigadier, I only ask that you read the files on this, review the plan, and consider my proposal. If you don't like it, we'll never talk again. But if you like what you see and want to move forward, give me a call."

"What about Liam and the Italians?" I asked her, wondering if her plan was remotely worthy of my review.

"Liam has considered it and is willing to come to the table. I'm still working on Mr. Bianchi, but we are also close to consideration from him." Her words were well-calculated and smooth.

She handed me the tablet and walked to the door.

***

All the rumors about Elise being brilliant are turning out to be true. She manages all the business and financial side of the cartel companies. An informant tells me she's managed to triple the amount of money laundered through the cartel's bars, not an easy or safe task when you're washing billions of dollars. It took me only thirty minutes to study her proposal before acknowledging she had created an excellent plan for us.

Dmitri might be used to getting any woman he wants, but Elise is different. I know Elise. My brother doesn't stand a chance.

Chapter Eight

DMITRI

I'm too pissed to enjoy myself tonight. In town for less than a week, and already, Andrei has me attending a black-tie event. He knows I hate fundraisers and shaking hands with people like the mayor. But I'll be Brigadier soon, and these events will be part of the new job. So reluctantly, I came.

Thinking about that reality makes me feel strange. Though I'm ready to be Brigadier—as I've been prepared for a higher position all my life—now that it's happening, it feels surreal. A lot of accountability comes with that position. I mean, look at Andrei.

I want to be Brigadier, but I don't want to be the current version of my brother. He's always in control of his actions and emotions, whereas my own preference is to loosen up a bit.

"Try and have a fun time, brother. Maybe you'll even find a nice lady to take home at the end of the evening." Andrei says that with a glimmer in his eyes and a friendly shove to my shoulder. He knows me a little too well.

"I just need a blow job in one of the bathrooms. No need to take her home. Perhaps I'll try the mayor's wife." I know how to irritate my brother, and touching influential men's wives is entirely off-limits in his book. It was a Savin lesson from our father that you don't mix business and pleasure, and it's a message Andrei has taken to heart. He gives me a stern look like a father would give his son while telling him to behave.

I leave him to shake the mayor's hand, take pictures, and chat with the guests. You know, the usual stuff. The more I do it, the more I realize why I hate it. This is a room full of selfish, high-functioning narcissists, all trying to act like friends when all they want is a way to fulfill their selfish desires. I guess this applies to me, too, but at least I try not to be so pretentious about it. As soon as an opening appears, I head straight to the bar.

"Vodka on the rocks." The very sexy young bartender smiles back at me. Maybe an after-party later with this one will make my evening better. I pause for a moment at that thought, my eyes on her while she makes my drink, but I quickly lose interest. Truth be told, there is someone on my mind. Someone who refuses to go away. *Elise.* I've been thinking about her.

At night, I lie awake, turning from one side to the other, restless and imagining her soft lips on mine. I smell the vanilla scent of her hair, hearing the sounds she made as she came on my cock.

Fuck! Why am I still thinking about her? But she has distracted my mind the past few days, filling all my fantasies as I stroked my cock these past few nights. It was supposed to be just sex, and that's still what it was. So why, then, do I find myself craving her? She wanted to push me away that night, but she let me take her. That slight resistance has fueled the flames in me.

Sipping my vodka, I survey the room with vague interest. Everything has been set up exquisitely, from the dazzling lights to the servers in their crisply ironed white and black uniforms. They circulate the room, visiting each attendee attentively and attending to the guests.

Guests are locked in conversations, laughing, whispering, shaking hands, and making fake inquiries about each other's well-being.

"Welcome home, my friend." Adam Brooks approaches the bar, raising his glass at me.

"Adam, nice to see you this evening."

This man always comes along with a charming grin and happy out-look. He acts as though someone has told him he resembles a famous person, so he leans into it, smiling, waving, and putting up this charming guy act. We went to high school together. His dad is a New York senator. And to those who don't know him, he appears to be the perfect son.

"I heard you were home. How's the family business?" he asks.

I shrug and sip my drink. "Keeping us busy as always. And you?"

"You haven't heard, Dmitri? I'm running for Senate when my father retires." He doesn't try to hide his pride. This prick is made for politics. It's like his birthright. He has all the right connections, having graduated from Yale at the top of his class and then moved on to Yale Law School. Ladies love his blond hair and blue eyes.

But I know the real Adam.

We partied in the same New York socialite circle in our younger days. Despite his beautiful Yale alum wife, he loves all the young girls and all the blow his nose can handle.

Well, we all have our vices. That's the very nature of men. Perhaps it's a true genetic weakness. Every man in this room has the one thing that brings him down on their knees behind closed doors. Even my brother, Andrei, and her name is Cora.

"Let me introduce you to a few friends." He waves me over to a bunch of guys.

Great, a bunch of middle-aged wealthy businessmen.

"It's good for business," he says and laughs. "I know you, Dmitri. Leave the pretty, young bartender to do her job, and let's talk about money." Adam's voice and constant talking make it impossible to think. He goes on and on about his friends, never letting up, never stopping to draw breath. This fool never shuts up.

Besides, we all know that his friends are only looking for what Adam can give them when he wins the election—and I do mean win. In New York, elections aren't a democracy. The elected officials are chosen by the rich and powerful men who fill this exact room tonight.

I know what Adam wants and why he's made it a point to let me know he's running for his father's Senate seat. He wants a donation check. Oh, he'll get one. And he knows I'll eventually call in a favor in return. That's how New York City works.

"Guys, this is Dmitri Savin, an old friend from high school," he says, formally introducing me to the group. The men take turns shaking my hand.

One of the men furrows his eyebrows. "Savin. Any relations to Andrei Savin?"

"Yes. He's my older brother."

"I should have known. The two of you look alike." The man chuckles.

Another laughs as well and says, "Andrei is a great guy."

The men around join us. It's almost like an initiation ritual, showing the things I'll have to start doing when I become Brigadier.

Anyone important enough to know in New York knows Andrei. I'm used to people asking if I'm related to him. As the leader of our family, he makes his way around the New York City business and social scenes, being part of New York's elusive and lavish elite circle here in Manhattan, people not part of the underworld. Our status in New York dates back to our grandfather, who came from Russia and made New York his home. The Savins are a well-known wealthy generational family. Or, as others call it, old money.

I sneak a smile to the bartender, who notices licking her lips. She's hot, but not Elise hot. Some time with her would take my mind off Elise, or perhaps I'll let her give me a blowjob and imagine it's Elise's lips on my cock.

But for now, I pretend to listen, nodding as the men talk, gulping my drink to get drunk as fast as possible, simply to tolerate this hellish evening.

Is there anything remotely interesting here? I check out a few escorts in their tight, short dresses. They don't shy away from smiling back if they notice me looking.

My eyes wander to the entrance, scouting for anyone else I might be interested in talking to. Before my eyes, like some apparition, Elise walks in. The sudden sight of her causes my lips to twist into a smile while an uncomfortable erection presses hard against my slacks.

Why is she here tonight?

Then I remembered she mentioned her status as a business leader in the city. What business does she represent, though? My eyes follow her, studying her every movement. She skips the line to shake the mayor's hand and make her way to the coffee bar. I can't help but laugh that she does the exact same thing as me.

She is stunning tonight, her hair falling over her shoulders in long curls while her makeup shimmers as though she's put extra effort into her appearance. Her black dress, so tight around her curves, leaves nothing to a man's imagination. I scan the room. I'm not the only one staring.

"Excuse me, gentlemen." I place my hand on Adam's shoulder and tilt my chin, indicating I have other business to address. He sees what I'm watching and doesn't object to my departure.

I don't walk up to her but decide to follow from a distance, to watch her, to admire from afar.

Chapter Nine

ELISE

"Yummy!" Jessica walks into my office, coffee in hand. "You'll be turning some heads tonight."

Turning to her, I reply, "I'm going for business, nothing more."

"Well, that's not going to stop all the guys from gawking at you and wanting to take you home."

Looking at myself again, I've gone a little overboard with my hair and makeup. "I'm not some treat for the men, Jessica," I correct her. "You must take note of that. You don't need validation from guys before you feel good about yourself."

I run a finger through my hair. "But I guess you're right. Men will be turning their heads."

I'm sure I'll see all the right players—the mayor, Mr. Bianchi, the Brigadier, and any other man hoping the few dollars he's contributed to the mayor's campaign will get him a favor. They all know who I am. They'll be watching me. It won't be bad if the picture they get is a nice one. Let them understand that a woman can compete with men without breaking her beauty.

That's not why I put the effort in tonight, though. The Savin brothers are part of New York City's elite high society circle that goes back generations. They've slowly built themselves into the city's foundation, guaranteeing their presence at these events, all part of their front.

Undoubtedly, the Brigadier will attend the fundraiser with his wife, Cora. But Dmitri is home, and he's also part of the city's high society. He doesn't strike me as the kind of man who'd want to attend these public events, but the thought of seeing him again makes my stomach hurt—and between my legs ache even more.

As excited as I am to see the man I've been thinking about for days, I must ensure he doesn't discover my identity. At least, not yet. However, if there's a slight chance he's there, I need to be the most beautiful woman in the room.

What if he doesn't remember me?

I take a deep breath, frowning, needing to get it together. I'm putting too much thought into a man I know I'm supposed to stay away from.

My thoughts of him are interrupted when my phone begins to vibrate.

My sister Alexis' number comes across my screen, and I immediately see Jessica's look of disapproval when I decline the call.

An hour later, Alejandro drops me off in front of the hotel. Guests have arrived in their couture and any piece of clothing that screams, 'I'm rich!' I won't even comment on the jewelry that, combined, amounts to the millions sitting in my offshore accounts. It's precisely what you'd expect at a gathering like this—people trying to outdo one another, showing off wealth.

I've opted for a simpler look with a short black dress and a diamond bracelet. My reputation already attracts enough attention.

Most of the guests walk in arms linked with their date for the night. Some are spouses, some mistresses, and a few are escorts. Since Liam is gone, I'm attending solo. Tonight, it is about business, not pleasure.

My mind brings up Dmitri again. *What if he's here and has brought a date?* Already, I hate that bitch, whoever she may be. I exhale deeply, intent on chasing that thought away.

I enter the hall and see the mayor standing with his wife, greeting guests as they enter the grand ballroom. I move to the right, skipping the eager line, waiting to be seen, shaking the mayor's hand, and getting their pictures in the newspaper. He knows who I am since I delivered the cash payment last month for his campaign. So, I'll skip the dull introductions. Thanks very much.

Over by the wall to which my senses pull me, there's an assortment of drinks. *Yes! Coffee!*

It's a simple pleasure for me to have a hot coffee instead of Champagne or wine, a calming effect that not everyone understands.

The waiter in uniform pours me a cup, and I decline their offer of sugar and cream.

Upon noticing the crowd, I feel myself retreating into my shell, not being too fond of these things. I don't belong here. I didn't grow up in New York City, didn't attend elite private schools, or even grew up with money. Tonight, it is about being rich and being seen with the right people, and neither crowd includes someone like me. So, when I come to these things, I usually let Liam take the lead and chat with the essential people while I watch from the sidelines.

But Liam is not here tonight. I am awkwardly solo, needing to attempt to mingle.

Everyone is putting on a show, after all. I can't be the exception, so I scan the room for a familiar face before finding one.

Andrei Savin exhibits money. He stands tall, dressed in a black suit, black button-down shirt, and black tie. His gold watch blings from across the room. In a room full of influential men, Andrei appears to be the most dominant.

Hailing from generations of wealth and Brigadiers, he's the Coalition's elite. To the ordinary New Yorker, Andrei is one of New York's over-privileged, high-society men who grew up in this city. He's wealthy, successful, and one of the most handsome men you'll ever see.

He's tall and dark, with black hair, hazel eyes, and ripped lean muscles. He and Dmitri look very much alike. Being the Brigadier, however, Andrei is more refined, whereas Dmitri looks like a killer. The Andrei glaring back at me screams power. Our eyes meet, and I brace myself, keeping a straight face as he casually walks over.

"I see Liam sent his girl tonight." I take displeasure at being called 'his girl' but don't dare to correct him.

"He couldn't make it." The words hiss through my teeth.

"You look lovely, Elise." Andrei's eyes move from my heels to my face. When it seems he likes what he sees, he smiles dashingly, and I instantly forgive him for his prior statement.

I offer a curt nod. "Thank you, Brigadier. You're not too bad yourself."

He laughs as a very confident man would.

"Don't be so stiff, Elise," he says. "Relax. You belong here. You've earned it."

"I don't doubt that," I say.

He smirks. "Looks like you want to disappear."

I look away from him nervously, knowing this man sees right through me. There's a spirit between Andrei and me. Although we're enemies by simply being part of the underworld life, Andrei has always shown me kindness while being stern with me.

I would be lying if I claimed not to think about how it would be to join the enemy, the Savins. The Savin men are all about family, including Cora and their mother. Unlike the cartel and Señor Martinez, they don't rule by placing fear in women because they don't have to.

But I'm cartel.

As long as Liam runs our U.S. operations, my loyalty is to him. For now, I enjoy my small moments with Andrei. "Maybe you're wrong."

I hate the fact that an enemy I hardly know affects me so much.

He dips his brow, but his eyes don't leave me. "Maybe I am."

A waiter walks up to him and offers him a glass of Champagne. He declines with a grimace, and the waiter nods slightly. Then, like a robot, the waiter ambles off to serve other guests.

Andrei's voice draws my attention. "I hear there was an issue with the permits getting approved?"

"No issue. I took care of it. Everything is set."

"I know you won't disappoint me, Elise." He has a glow of admiration on his face.

Smiling, I promise him, "I won't."

He stares at me for a moment, his lips pressing into a fine line, his body tensing before my eyes. It's as though there's lust in his gaze. I hope Dmitri didn't say something to him. He makes me self-conscious, my head turning shyly.

He cuts into the silence. "Enjoy your evening, Elise." Quickly, he turns around, walking through the crowd, shaking hands, and saying good evening to several associates.

Left standing there alone again, not wanting to overthink my interaction with Andrei, I walk around the room, sipping my coffee and watching the crowd talk and drink. People tend to talk more when they have alcohol inside them, so it's always good to stay sober and listen to what they're saying to eavesdrop on something of interest.

"Elise Walsh." The voice is soft and beautiful, a pleasant change from the brashness of the voices surrounding me. It's also very familiar.

I turn around to see another beautiful woman from my world working tonight.

"Good evening, Ivy. Surprised to see you here."

Ivy Kelley is quite the spitfire, super intelligent, very sexy, and a whole lot of crazy. That makes her the most dangerous female assassin in New York City and one of the few I call my friend.

Her glossy lips part as she responds, "Work. I'd ask you, but I know you're working as well. You should enjoy a drink and put the coffee cup down."

I shake my head with a giggle. *She's probably right.*

She eyes me over and nods approvingly. "You're looking beautiful tonight."

"Says the one turning heads," I respond with a soft laugh. Ivy is the hottest woman I know. Her dark red hair, fair skin, and gorgeous body make men drop to their knees and bend at her will.

She waves her hand, showing off a neat manicure, and winks at me. "The men think they've got us all figured out, Elise. Little do they know that we are the ones they should fear, not the other men in this room."

I can't help but acknowledge she's right, so I chuckle at the statement. We are significantly underestimated in this world.

"I saw you talking to Andrei earlier. You know his brother Dmitri is back in town?" she whispers as if we're two teenage girls gossiping.

"Yes, I know." My words burst out faster than intended, almost defensive.

She twirls a fine silver necklace around her finger. "I wouldn't mind getting some of that Savin brother action. He's a very handsome man."

I'm weirdly annoyed by her statement. Dmitri is mine! I don't like her talking about him in this way, my gut lurching with jealousy. This reaction within my mind startles me, but I still hold firmly to it, regardless. *What is wrong with me?*

She starts laughing, her eyes crinkling, deeply amused. "I see someone's got a crush."

"What? I don't even know him." I find myself trying to convince both her and me, my tone unexpectedly sharp as if she irritates me.

"Don't worry, Elise. If I drop to my knees for any Savin brother, the Colonel is more my taste."

Her eyes narrow for a second, then she says casually, "Well, my mark is on the move, so I'm out of here. Nice seeing you again."

"Goodnight, Ivy. Be safe."

"You, too." She disappears among the crowd.

I continue to make my way around the room, smiling at men and saying hello to their wives.

Walking through a crowd of boring businesspeople making promises they don't intend to keep, I immediately halt, finding someone waiting for me. Standing in front of me with beautiful hazel eyes is the best-looking man in the room.

Dmitri!

Chapter Ten

DMITRI

My heart speeds up with every minute of watching her, craving to be near her, to touch her, claim her.

"Elise," I call out.

She stops, turning to me. The image of my cock thrusting in and out of her plays back in my mind, forceful and intense. It makes me lascivious and hard, day and night, whenever it even flickers through my mind's eye.

The red on her lips also makes me want to devour them. I could forget I'm in a room full of people and get lost in her right now.

"Good evening," she says as though expecting me.

I restrain myself from reaching out to pull her to me.

"I'm surprised to see you here tonight. You look gorgeous." Her face and that pretty smile mesmerize me. I like seeing her show emotion, even just a smile, not her expressionless face when she meets other people.

"Thank you." She glances around as though looking for someone.

"Are you here alone?" I ask, pretty sure I already know the answer. I've been watching her. No man would want to leave the side of a woman as beautiful as Elise, not when there are men like me lurking around, trying to snatch her for themselves.

"Yes," she answers as she rubs her finger against her coffee cup. It is almost suggestive, or at least I like to think it is. Still, my mind refuses to lose the imagery of what we did and what we enjoyed together.

"Me too," I say, tapping my forehead as if something's slipped my mind. "Well, my brother and his wife are here, so I guess I'm not alone. Saw you talking to him earlier."

"Who's your brother?" She becomes expressionless again.

"Andrei," I blurt out, answering with a sharp tone. I love my brother, but the thought of Elise being anywhere near him is abhorrent in a world where I'm constantly compared to him. She should get to know me only as Dmitri, the man who fucked her hard and left his cum inside of her, not as Andrei's brother.

"Oh. Yes, he asked me if the coffee was good." She sips her drink while those delectable eyes look up and bore into mine, seeing how I react.

"You do like your coffee." She's unlike any other women I've slept with, testing my control.

"If you'll excuse me," she says, suddenly cutting herself off and turning to leave, but I don't want her to. She hesitates as if expecting me to say something and, at the same time, averts her gaze when I take hers in. "I just need some fresh air."

"Yeah, me too. These functions are quite stale." With a smirk, I point at a group of wealthy men locked in hearty conversation, laughing and sipping their drinks. "Take a look at those guys. You'd think they're all best friends, but it's all one crazy show. I sometimes get sick of it."

"You get it," she says, chuckling.

Did I just make her laugh?

"I do. Let me walk you out." I gently grab her arm before she has a chance to object to the offer. We sidle past the crowd, leaving through a side door. Outside, the alleyway is dark, and there isn't anyone around. The air is cool, and the calmness is a bit unsettling.

"It's dark tonight," I say, which sounds remarkably stupid, given that the nights are always dark. The real darkness is men like me lurking about this evening.

Her neck twitches, and her body tenses. "I'm not afraid of the dark if that's what you're thinking."

Hmm, so she says.

My hand is still resting on her arm. "Everyone has something that terrifies them and keeps them awake."

"So, what keeps you awake at night?" she says coyly, holding my gaze.

"I'm what keeps people awake at night." Her iris glistens as though she understands my statement, but she's not scared of me at all. Instead, she seems curious.

"And you?" I ask her.

"Failure," she blurts out with an expressionless face again. I have no doubt she means it. Something about her reminds me of myself. Dearly, I wish these blank expressions of hers would stop occurring when she's with me. It's like some switch she can flick off, making me jittery when she shifts from warm and chatty to cool and dismissive.

She shivers slightly when a brush of freezing air drifts by. I want to wrap my jacket around her shoulder, but she's a strong woman and would see it as a sign of weakness.

"Are you cold?" She rapidly shakes her head, muttering softly, and I swear that a hint of a scowl crosses her brow.

We stay silent for a moment as we walk down the dark and quiet alleyway. "I can walk you to your car. It doesn't seem safe out here," I offer.

Again, she dismisses me. "That's okay. I got it. Thank you."

I stand there and linger, rubbing my hands behind my neck. "Well, you have a good evening, Elise."

"You too," she replies and turns to walk away.

Those lips are too inviting to let Elise leave tonight without kissing her. So, my body lurches forward, making a grab for her wrist to pull her close, placing my other hand around her waist.

Our eyes lock, and in that fleeting moment, so many emotions flash through her eyes—fear, curiosity, bravery, and, most unexpected of all, vulnerability. Breathing deeply, I pull her close and crash my lips into hers.

Our kiss is aggressive. Her warm and wet tongue licks my lips as my teeth sink into her bottom lip. Her sweet little cry from my bite makes my mind and cock grow more strained.

I gently push against her body, forcing her to walk backward until her back hits the side of the building, and she's pinned between me and the wall. My kisses move down her neck, shoulder, and cleavage. She smells so good, tastes so delicious, and feels amazing in my arms.

I can tell her inner thighs are wet by how her needy moan sounds with every kiss placed on her body. My hands rub her ass as I lift her dress, feeling her silky thong and smooth, soft ass under my fingertips. "Elise."

"Yes." I feel the explosion of desire in her voice, the way it shakes.

"I'm going to fuck you." Lifting her leg with my arm, I place it around my right hip, her thighs open.

"Yes, please," she moans. My fingers slide into her pussy as she rocks her ass to match my rhythm. I continue to kiss and lick her, nibbling on her ears and chin.

"I wasn't asking for permission." Turning her around, I spread her legs, raising her hands against the wall. "Don't move," I whisper in her ear.

Dropping to my knees, my hands glide over her ass, and with both hands, I slip down her panties and spread her ass cheeks to admire her wet asshole. She pants as she anticipates my next move. Circling her anus with my tongue, I lick it like ice cream as my finger massages her clit.

Her body tenses at first but relaxes the more she trusts me to touch her, to own her. One hand playing with her pussy, my other hand rubs against her lower back. I flatten the top of my tongue against her asshole, getting her wetter and giving more pressure from every lick.

She rocks her ass against my tongue until cum starts dripping from her pussy. Midway through her coming, I quickly pull out my fingers, stand up, and turn her around. Looking into her eyes, I see a sparkle of excitement as I start to unzip my pants.

I lift her leg around my waist. "I've been a good boy all night. It's time for my reward."

She inches her waist against my cock. Her wetness from her cum makes it easy to push my cock inside her. Pounding her against the wall as hard as I can, she takes me all in.

"Oh, God!" Her cries get louder with every thrust.

"God can't save you from me," I growl.

The anticipation of this moment played in my head over the past few days makes it hard to stop my cock from busting within a few minutes.

Grabbing her ass with my left hand, I push her body against mine even harder. My cock is about to explode, but I need to hear her come again before letting it happen.

I release her ass cheeks that I've been grabbing aggressively and start circling her asshole with my finger. Her slit is so wet that I move some of the wetness to her ass and slide the top of my finger inside. It's obvious her ass hasn't been penetrated before from just seeing the surprise on her face. Her mouth opens, and a slight whimper of pain comes out.

She digs her nails deeper into my shoulder, but I ignore the pain, slamming her against the wall and sticking my finger further into her ass.

It's me and her up against this wall, with no care in the world about what or who may be around us. I'm completely lost in her, physically and emotionally. My body enjoys seeing her face moan in ecstasy, a piece of me embedded deep in both of her holes. My mind is consumed by every part of her, every move, every expression, and every sound, completely and utterly feeling something toward the woman in front of me. What that is, I don't know yet.

As I stare into her, a rush of liquid reaches my tip, Elise's eyes fluttering as she comes all over my cock. "Dmitri!" she cries.

Feeling her is a drug, and it's only a few more seconds before my cum is dripping out from inside her, all the way down her inner thighs, some of it spattering onto the ground.

I lean my arms on the wall behind her, breathing hard, not wanting my time with her to end. But she cuts the moment short, her face flushed red as she comes down from her orgasm. Before I can grab her and tell her to stay with me, she starts running down the alley, positioning her clothes back in place, not looking back, and disappearing around the corner.

She's running from me.

Chapter Eleven

ELISE

As usual, the smell of coffee fills the air. Jessica places a steaming mug neatly by my side. "Elise, you look stressed."

I glance at my hot brew, letting the steam waft over my face. *Soothing.*

"Not stressed, just busy. Today is a big day." I sip my coffee and review the contracts that need to be signed shortly. "Is everything taken care of for lunch at Flamiche?" I don't even peek up from the paperwork on my desk to address her.

"Yes. I reserved a table in the middle of the restaurant," she assures me.

"And Diego?"

"He and security have completed perimeter checks and will be there."

That's all I need right now—top-notch efficiency. I can always depend on Jessica for that.

"Thanks. I need the men to play nice today. I need this deal to go through," I say, crossing my fingers.

Jessica understands a lot is riding on this deal. "I know. You've been working hard for months on it. It will go through. Everyone knows you created a great plan."

Tapping my pen on the desk, thinking about everything laid out before me and how the past few months have been, I let out a deep sigh.

"I need to do better, Jessica. Be better. And remember, when I move up, so do you."

"Don't be too hard on yourself, Elise. You're doing amazing." She gives such a good pep talk. I need it. Jessica is one of the few people I trust. This sentiment does not come easily to our cartel life, so you hold onto it when you find it with someone.

Jessica was a bartender when I started having her help me out around the office. She was intelligent, quick, and completely loyal, so I promoted her to my assistant. Within six months, she went from making two hundred dollars a night in tips to two hundred thousand dollars a year, plus a bonus.

Plus, she likes women, so I don't have to worry about her disappearing during work to rendezvous with the cartel men in the back offices.

"You're right," I say, and she beams.

"Tell Alejandro to have the vehicle ready." Opening my tablet, I review the plans for today's meeting.

Being Liam's third-in-command doesn't mean anything unless you're in the cartel. I've spent the last few years solidifying my place in his business. Lately, I've begun to feel a little trapped. Señor Martinez's dislike for me blocks me from being able to work in other operations of the cartel throughout the U.S., so I need a way to expand myself here in New Jersey and New York. Looking for an opportunity, a problem has fallen right in my lap.

One evening, the men were downstairs in the bar, having a round of tequila for the soldiers we had just lost in a shootout at the port. One of the men who died was Diego's brother. I inquired about the port situation, deciding to investigate the issue further, learning about the war between the different organized crime fractions over port space.

It took me months of researching and educating myself on all there was to know about the ports and the shipments received through them before I could draft a plan that would benefit all three families. Many hours and sleepless nights were spent creating a perfect deal that led to today's meeting.

I want to use this deal with the three families to expand within the under-ground world across the northeast and the U.S., moving from the men seeing me as the 'cartel woman' to 'Elise, a boss.' My future career plans start with transforming the ports.

Having spent the last forty-eight hours thinking about my time with Dmitri in the alley, I now find myself behind in my work, with far too much at stake. I cannot afford any distractions at this stage. This is the first time I've given a man this much attention, and I remind myself, again, that it needs to stop.

A long time ago, I promised myself that a man would never be a priority or distract me from my goal of becoming a boss.

Most importantly, part of this promise was that a man would never make my decisions for me. Yet a man does make my decisions, something that aggrieves me immensely. I'm just not sleeping with the man concerned. I'm only able to make a move with Liam's permission.

My distrust of men started a long time ago. Growing up in a trailer park in a town south of Seattle, the skies were always gloomy around there. Overcrowded, the park we lived in was full of drug dealers and addicts, every corner spelling danger, with nasty characters lurking and watching me like predators. It became a place that wasn't safe for me as a teenage girl. The lingering gazes from scrawny men and their leering each time any young girl walked by were hard to deal with. It went beyond stares sometimes, and some of the girls were assaulted.

I never showed them my fear, secretly having a knife attached to my thigh, just in case. I've been around danger my whole life but never considered myself a victim. I will fight to my death.

I never knew my father and can't even be sure my mom knows who he is.

When I was growing up, there was always some new guy she was dating, someone who'd hang around for a few months. Then, she'd introduce me to a new one right after. That was my mom. She fell in love quickly and hard, and after a few months of him taking care of her and us, they quickly dumped her.

But that's okay. She'd have a new boyfriend right after.

Not wanting to be around her and them as a teenager, I spent most of my time studying in the local coffee shop. When I was old enough, I got a job there to help pay for college, plus I got a discount on my coffee. That coffee shop became my second home, quiet and comfortable, a place to find solitude with myself and my thoughts. Drinking coffee reminds me of that place and the feeling of safety, giving me a sense of belonging. So, of course, the first thing I bought when I made my first million dollars was that coffee shop.

My mom always told her boyfriends about me, saying, "She's smart, she's going to college. She'll make it big someday." She was right. I saved money for college and worked hard studying at school to get straight A's. The day after graduation, I flew to New York.

In the city, I'd be able to create a new life for myself, not having to hear people talk about my mother and feel sorry for me for being her child. I loved my mom; she always tried her best. But her best was not *my* best. I used the words people said about her as motivation to work hard so that I could one day leave and create a new home for myself.

In New York City, I'm Elise Walsh, Mexican cartel boss. In Seattle, I was only white trash with a slutty mother. Graduation day was the last time I saw her.

One night, she went out for drinks and wrapped the front bumper around a tree off I-5, where she perished on the spot. I didn't return to see her body. Instead, after a neighbor identified her, I had her cremated and spread her ashes in the Puget Sound so that she could continue living freely in spirit.

I vowed never to return to Seattle in this lifetime. It's a promise I intend to keep.

My phone rings. Jessica knows I'm deep in thought and busy working, so she moves to answer the call. Instead, in front of me, she declines it.

"Your sister keeps calling," Jessica whispers.

"Please don't mention that to the guys."

My sister Alexis showed up in New Jersey shortly after me, wanting nothing from me but my time. Since our mother died, it's been just the two of us. I offered her money to return to Seattle, but she declined. The more I pressed her to return home, the more she worked to stay. Being determined, she's been making her own mark in the underground world, the life I wanted to shield her from, but she saw it as a playground for power and money.

No one knows about my sister except a few people I consider friends. For her safety, I need her to stay away from me and the cartel business. If Señor Martinez or other players found out about her, they could use her to hurt me. So, instead of calling her, I continue avoiding her calls and ignoring her altogether.

Chapter Twelve

ELISE

Flamiche is elegant and traditional, and the menu is full of great-tasting food, not that anyone will eat at the meeting. The three invited influential men will sit and enjoy a bottle of wine, which they'll watch being brought to the table, asking for it to be opened in front of them to ensure its safety. But they won't eat for fear of being poisoned.

It is, of course, a tight interweaving of fate that has brought all three men together, and no one intends to split this odd connection. They are not friends, and they certainly don't trust each other. But, somehow, I have convinced them to work together for money. And money—vast sums of it—is always good enough.

Cartel snipers have been placed across the street in case something goes wrong and one of the men decides to change the course of the meeting. They will also watch for federal agents who might find out about our meeting and want to stop by. There can't be loose ends, and I've ensured there won't be any of those either.

Big days like this have a nasty habit of going wrong with a lack of planning. Fail to plan, and you plan to fail—as everyone knows.

Making my way into the room, I see a table in the far-left corner occupied by two Mexican men having lunch, obviously cartel. The men blend in nicely, talking in hushed tones, not making eye contact, and trying to act inconspicuously.

Another table across the room has a few Italian men sitting around it, also locked in hushed conversation, acting naturally—Mr. Bianchi's men. And, of course, a few Russian men are strategically positioned in the other corner to protect the Brigadier.

But I've reserved a table in the center of the room, hoping that being in a busy restaurant at the same time as New York City workers enjoying their lunch will make all these volatile men behave. I don't expect any trouble, not today, but I am always prepared for it.

"Hola, Liam," I say, greeting my boss with a hug and a wide smile. I haven't seen or talked to him much since Houston, but he's assured me there's nothing to worry about. I have no other choice but to believe him.

"Elise, you've been busy. How was the fundraiser?"

I shrug. "Uneventful. The mayor saw me, and I delivered a contribution."

"Good. Let's hope today goes well for you and all of us." I watch his face and try to understand his meaning, but he moves to sit in the seat to my right.

Next, Mr. Bianchi walks in, a big Italian guy, heavy around the waist, always smelling of cigars.

"Mr. Bianchi, pleased to see you today," I say, attempting to shake his hand.

"Elise, ciao." He shifts my hand out of the way and wraps his arms around me, lifting me slightly off the ground. His arms are warm and friendly, his voice hearty. Unlike Liam and Andrei, who are cold and unwelcoming, Mr. Bianchi makes you feel like family until the gun is pressing into your back.

Mr. Bianchi comes from a line of Cosa bosses, the head of the five Italian Mob families who run the East Coast. So, even though the man always hugs me when he sees me, I am fully aware of how dangerous he is and always proceed with caution.

When I first introduced the deal to him at Luigi's Spaghetti Restaurant, where he and his men are headquartered, I knew there was a chance of not walking out alive.

However, significant risks equal big rewards, and the risk is worth it. The FBI has arrested his Italian soldiers, so I lean into the fact that Mr. Bianchi will have decided he can use less killing in his current business dealings.

A few minutes later, the Brigadier joins us. I'm sure arriving last is a power play.

I catch his attention. "Brigadier, nice to see you this afternoon."

"Elise," he greets me as he walks over to his seat and lowers himself.

Though always extremely cautious when dealing with the Brigadier, today, I feel different, but in a bad way, almost more afraid of him.

My recent endeavors with Dmitri have caused me to feel as though I'm betraying Andrei and our business relationship. If he were to find out about Dmitri and me, this business relationship would end with me shackled in their basement. Everyone in the underworld has heard the vilest stories about that place, another kind of 'underworld,' a tasteless pun if you like. The basement is where you experience pain so scrutinizing that you beg for a bullet.

But I'm betraying Liam. As far as he's concerned, Dmitri is the enemy, and I've slept with him. Dmitri has become my vice. The thing you know is bad for you and may destroy you, but you can't stop it, like a hard drug. Shelving those thoughts, it's vital to stay focused on the moment.

"Well, men, we know why we're here today. We have details to finalize and contracts to sign."

Each man opens his folder, flipping through the documents the lawyers have already reviewed.

The waiter approaches slowly. She asks, "Can I get you something to drink or eat?"

"We'll take a bottle of Saint's red, please. Open it at the table." When I return my attention to the men in front of me, the waiter scurries away to the bar.

Each man watches as I take charge. They might be the bosses, but this is my plan, my meeting.

I start to talk about the various contracts, status updates, and action plans for the upcoming deal. A few questions come my way, but the three barely speak to each other.

Things are going well as we finalize the paperwork, and the men quickly empty the bottle of wine. Then, Liam speaks up, and my heart stops for two seconds.

"Are we sure this deal is the right path forward?"

His words hit me like a sucker punch. He's been acting a bit strangely today, and somewhere deep in the dark crevices of my mind, something whispers fear into me. I'd shrugged it off because it was Liam, having already got his backing on the deal. But hearing those words now sends a ripple through the air and a frisson of cold nerves down my spine.

This moment is precisely why I arranged this meeting at a busy restaurant. If it weren't, then by now, bullets would be flying before any questions would come.

Liam should know that, so why this question?

"Are you backing out?" Andrei puts down his glass of wine, glaring at Liam with fire in his hazel eyes. His lips curl aggressively, and his eyes flash with wrath. Liam remains calm and unmoved by the outburst. Not one to be afraid of the Russians, he equally stares back.

Trying to break the ice, I quickly ask, "Liam, is there something wrong that we need to address before moving forward?"

A low laugh escapes him as though he's just heard a joke. "No, Elise."

"Well, is everyone on board? Are we finalizing in a few weeks?" I look at each of the men. They all shake their heads in agreement to close the deal.

"Okay, gentlemen. I think we have what we need. You enjoy the rest of your day." I stand up to conclude the meeting.

Liam and Mr. Bianchi quickly say their goodbyes and leave while each of the men at the other tables stands and starts to walk out right behind them. Andrei, however, is slower.

Our eyes meet, and I offer a smile. "Brigadier."

"I'll walk you out, Elise." He motions for us to move toward the door.

I keep my calm, trying not to give off any more uncertain vibes. Liam's question has rattled everyone, and Andrei must now have doubts.

"Do I need to be worried, Elise?" His voice is troubled with a hint of anger.

"I don't see why, Brigadier." I attempt to sound confident, but Andrei sees right through me.

Before responding in a growl, he considers my response for a short while. "Then what the fuck was Liam's comment about?"

"I don't know, but I assure you the cartel is in for the deal."

"Elise, they better be. For your sake!"

The man giving me a stern look is not the Andrei who, just days ago, eyed me with lust. The man I stand in front of is a powerful and brutal one, the Brigadier.

Fear ripples through me, although I don't show it. Questions burn. What happened in Houston?

The Brigadier turns as his black vehicle pulls up to the curb. His driver gets out to open his door.

"Bye, Elise." He still sounds angry, but when his eyes meet mine, a look of pity falls on me. He pauses before getting into the vehicle. Towering over me, his finger brushes the side of my forehead as he tucks a stray hair behind my ear, his touch oddly gentle for a man who just scolded me moments ago.

My heart skips a beat, feeling something unfamiliar for the man in front of me. However, whatever it is, it's not close to what I feel for his brother.

Hearing a door open, I shake off the moment and draw my attention to the other man getting out of the vehicle. I turn around, locking eyes with a man all too familiar.

"Hello, Elise," the man holding the gun says to me.

Chapter Thirteen

DMITRI

I watch Elise through the window having lunch with the men. She leads the meeting as though she's equal to the three bosses. They trust her. Andrei is known to only trust a handful of people, so his confidence in a woman working for our enemy is interesting. I came today to protect Andrei, but seeing her is a bonus, especially now that I know who she is. I still haven't decided what to do with my Elise yet.

After leaving the fundraiser, I went straight to my office. She knew my name, calling me Dmitri when she came on my cock. I repeatedly replayed the moment in my head, making sure I hadn't imagined it.

After digging, there she was—my girl—Elise Walsh. An online search shows she's a twenty-five-year-old Chief Operating Officer for The Martinez Tequila Bar Corporation, and her résumé is quite impressive. Through hard work, a girl from the trailer park in Seattle made her way up to third-in-command for the Martinez Cartel's U.S. operations. Not only is she young, but she's also the only woman and non-Mexican heritage boss in the cartel.

I knew there was something about her the first night we met. The competition would have been riveting if we'd been just two businesspeople in New York City. But we aren't ordinary people, hailing from a world of crime and sins. She's the cartel woman. She's the enemy.

The driver pulls the vehicle to the curb. As he jumps out to open the door for Andrei, I watch Andrei and Elise in the side mirror. At first, I don't move. He is scolding her, something I'm familiar with. But then, he does the unexpected. He tucks a piece of her hair behind her ear.

Andrei doesn't go around touching other women. He's loyal to Cora, but this seems different.

Jealousy rages inside me, and without thinking, I jump out of the vehicle, gun in hand. I'm not sure who I intend the gun for. Is it for Elise, for lying to me, or my brother, Andrei, for touching what belongs to me?

Immediately after standing on the sidewalk, I see I have made a bad mistake. Andrei lowers his head at me as he enters the vehicle, leaving Elise all alone.

Hearing me, she turns around, eyes wide open.

"Hello, Elise," I say. She bites on her lip as if keeping certain words inside. She sighs.

It seems I've stunned her. Wrestling with my anger toward both her and my brother, I decide the best thing to do is retreat. Without acknowledging the two of them, I slide back into the vehicle, signaling to the driver that we need to move.

As we pull away, I watch her still standing on the sidewalk, looking my way, fearful. I'm angry, feeling betrayed. *So, why am I sitting here beating myself up for frightening her?*

Even after finding out who she was, I couldn't stop thinking about her, images replaying in my mind of fucking her in the alleyway as I stroked my cock in the shower. I often picture her biting her bottom lip, which she frequently does when we're together. A woman I've known for a week has sparked more of a response from me than all the women I've met combined. Now, I am fighting my urge to take her into my possession because I must stay away.

In the mirror, Andrei's eyes stare back.

Is he upset because I might know her or because I've interrupted his time with her?

What bad luck that out of all the women I could be fucking in New York City, the one woman Andrei has told me is off-limits is the one I can't stop thinking about. He won't take me disobeying his orders lightly, even if it's a mistake. *Damn it!* A future Brigadier doesn't make mistakes. There will be consequences for my disobedience.

When the vehicle pulls up to El Grande, I hastily make my way to my condo, never asking Andrei how his meeting today has gone. Right now, I don't care.

The empty condo I came home to last week still has hardly any furniture, food, or anything else, making it resemble a home. But at least now I have a bottle of vodka in which to drown my worries tonight. I uncap the bottle and take a sip, not needing a glass because I intend to finish all of it, the entire liter.

I sit in my armchair, sulking as the skyline turns dark, taking a few more sips of vodka.

It must be the drink because something seems to be drawing me to the splash of colors in the sky. I almost picture myself watching the sunset with Elise by my side, drowning in the beauty of everything together.

Fuck!

One of the men walks in. "Leave me alone," I grunt, not turning.

"Dmitri." Andrei's voice startles me slightly.

I tilt my head back and pour more vodka down my throat. "What do you want?"

"You want to talk about what's going on with you?" The look of disapproval on his face sears into the back of my head as he stands behind me, staring, irritated.

"Nothing. Just need a drink, that's all."

He pauses, then asks, "Do you know Elise?"

I shouldn't lie to my brother, but I'm not ready to tell him about her. "No."

"This deal will be good for us."

What I actually hear in his tone is, 'Be the Brigadier, but make sure you follow my directions.'

So, my reply is, "I'm aware and won't be getting in the way."

"If becoming a Brigadier is too much—"

"It's not. I'm ready for it." I cut him off.

"Let me know if you need anything."

His hand momentarily rests on my shoulder, and he begins to walk away. There is something I must voice, however. "The cartel woman, Elise. Is she more than a business transaction?" My voice indicates a hint of jealousy.

Without warning, knuckles hit the side of my face, sending me slumping back. I catch his next punch with my hand and head-butt him, causing him to fall back. I quickly stand, ready to face off with Andrei. If it's a fight he wants, I'm ready, staring at my brother, knuckles clenched.

"Boys!" A woman's loud voice breaks the tension, a pregnant Cora standing at my door. "Andrei, dinner is ready."

I instantly regret my question. Cora is like a sister to me, and I hope I did not offend her.

"Coming, kitten." Andrei takes a few steps back from me.

Before exiting my condo, he turns and says, "Consider that a warning, Dmitri. The next time you disrespect me, you'll wish all I did was punch you." Straightening his tie, he walks out of my front door, following his wife.

I sit in silence after he leaves. It's been a long time since we've fought. We are close, so as much as I ruffle his feathers, he still wins my respect as head of our family and a Coalition Brigadier.

Today is different. My brother needs to know he can't touch what belongs to me. He doesn't know yet that I've marked her, but he will soon.

The bottle is half empty as I continue sitting and thinking about Elise, replaying when we met at the bar. Things would have played out differently if I'd known who she was.

Stroking my chin, I sip from the bottle again, my jaw slack, the drink pinching harder than usual.

Elise, what were you doing at the bar at midnight? You don't even live near this part of the city.

It can't be a coincidence that we met that night unless she planned it. Did she follow me there?

She had to know who I was already. And the more I think about the way she entered the bar, her eyes focused on her surroundings, the more I realize my big mistake. It's not that she didn't notice me; she purposely ensured that I noticed she didn't.

Dammit! She's outplayed me.

When I saw her talking to Andrei that night at the fundraiser, she lied to me, saying he had asked her about the coffee. What they were really talking about was the deal. Thinking about it, he looked at her with desire in his eyes as though he knew her.

The more I stew in thoughts and questions, the more I drink. The more I drink, the deeper in my thoughts I wallow. Hell, I wasn't always the enemy. I wasn't always this man.

***

"Happy Birthday Dmitri," Brigadier Valentin said as he walked me through the basement of El Grande. I had never been down here before. It was dark and scary.

"Thanks, Valentin," I replied, curious about where he was taking me. We stopped in front of a steel door.

He placed his hand on my shoulder. "You're thirteen today, so I have a present for you."

Though excited to see what he'd brought for me, I was still confused about why we had to come to the basement to get it.

He opened the door, gesturing for me to step through. When I did, I found a bloodied man sitting in a chair, tied up, no one else around. This wasn't the first time I had seen a man beaten or even dead, but still... What did he have to do with my birthday gift?

He walked me to the man, and we stood right before him. I couldn't stop staring. He was massive, looking brutish and intimidating.

Valentin placed something into my hand, metal on my fingers. I looked down. He had placed a gun in my grip. "Valentin, I don't understand. What am I doing here?"

I tried to step back, but he stopped me.

"Dmitri, Andrei had his first kill on his thirteenth birthday. And Nikolai, well, he's on a different path. Like your brother, I thought you would want the same present."

He wasn't trying to be cruel. Valentin was—and still is—my father's best friend and Andrei's godfather. He had always shown me love and support.

"I don't want to kill anyone." I tried to hand him back the gun. But he didn't take it.

"What do you mean, Dmitri? You're a Savin. You'll be part of the Coalition one day. You need to know what it's like to take a man's life."

"But Andrei is the future Brigadier, not me. I don't have to be part of the Coalition," I cry out, trying to hold back tears.

"Then what do you plan to do?" He was trying to understand me.

"I'm going to run the Savin business for Andrei. I don't need to be part of the Bratva to be a businessman." I had always been smart. Numbers came easy to me.

Since grade school, our private school placed me in advanced studies. My father did not intend to teach me about our family's business. Andrei was our future leader, the one who would control all our assets. But, when it was evident that I was brighter than Andrei and picked up financial information and business strategy at an early age, he had me join the two of them.

"That's all good, but you still need to know how to kill a man. Your last name makes this necessary." He lifted the gun in my hand and pointed it at the man. My hands jittered.

"Pull the trigger, Dmitri," he whispered in my ear.

But I couldn't. Terrified, I threw the gun down and ran toward the door and down the hall, Valentin's footsteps thudding behind me as his hand grabbed me. "We'll try again another time." He comforted me, his arms curling around me, embracing me in a hug.

There was a sense of relief until a loud bang rang through my ears. Valentin hit the ground on his knees, blood splashing on my face.

When I looked up, the tied-up man was holding the gun I had thrown. Before he could aim it at me next, I dropped to Valentin's side, grabbed his gun, and shot the man.

The Coalition and our family almost lost a Brigadier because I couldn't pull the trigger. A mistake I never let happen again.

***

I've drowned in vodka and my thoughts long enough to watch the sunrise. Tiredness begins to sink in, and my eyes start getting heavy, but I'm still fired up and in a drunken state. I stand up and throw the bottle across the room. The glass hits the wall, and pieces fly through the air, spreading across the floor like sparkling sand on a beach.

I turn, hearing a knock cut through my loud breathing.

Opening the door, I'm expecting to find Andrei, but instead, a tall blonde stands in front of me. "Can I get you anything, boss?" Stephanie, one of our business secretaries, walks into my condo uninvited. She's the daughter of one of the Coalition's associates and grew up with us.

We dated before I left for Russia. Spreading her naked body across my desk, I would snort a line of coke off her breasts while my cock was in her. It was a fun time. But that was long ago.

"You missed a good party last night," she says, her voice husky.

Her finger slides up my arm as she inches her body into mine.

"I told you I don't party like that anymore." I step back from her, walking into my office.

Following me, she shoots back, "I miss the old Dmitri."

I'm not in the mood for Stephanie's antics right now. "There is something you can do."

Her excitement is bubbling through her as her eyes widen and her cheeks flush. She thinks we are about to rekindle what we had three years earlier, that I'm going to lift her and pin her against the wall, shred her dress, and fuck her. But I've already told her those days are over.

Instead, I lean over my desk, brushing my arm over her side, pick up a piece of paper, and write *Elise Walsh* and the address of the tequila bar's headquarters. I place the paper in her hand, letting the touch linger. "Please send some expensive roses to this address. And have the card say, 'See you soon.'"

I walk over to my bar and take one last gulp of liquor.

"I told you, Stephanie, I'm not that guy anymore."

Staggering out of my office, I head to my bedroom to sleep through the hangover alone, needing to be ready for tonight.

Elise Walsh, I'm coming for you.

Chapter Fourteen

ELISE

I knew this moment would come, the moment Dmitri would realize I worked for the cartel, his enemy. But I wasn't expecting it yesterday, not during my meeting with his brother.

There was so much anger on his face. He also seemed upset at Andrei, but I'm not sure why.

I've only known him for a brief period, yet I've felt more alive in that time than for years. Barely dating and constantly diving into work, I didn't realize how good it was to be touched and desired anymore.

Now, I find myself lusting for a man I barely know, everything about him consuming me. When not in his presence, my mind is thinking of him. I dream of him while lying in bed at night, touching myself, remembering our time together.

That night in the alley, I felt everything between us, his eyes peering through me as though I were the only woman in the world. I could hear the loud sound of his heartbeat through his chest and drowned in it.

It's hard to explain the spark, but it's something wild and exciting.

Today, I woke up feeling different, feeling regret that I never should have followed him, never should have walked into the bar, letting the wetness between my legs overpower any rationale.

How did he find out my identity, though? At this point, it doesn't matter. He simply knows it, and now I must deal with any fallout from my hasty decision.

I stare at my tablet, not even working, just sipping coffee, lost in thoughts.

"Did you meet someone at the fundraiser?" Jessica says as she walks into my office, holding red roses. The wrap crunches in her hands, and she stares admiringly at them.

"No. Who is that from?" They're beautiful and definitely expensive.

"I don't know, but the card says, 'See you soon!'" She places the flowers in front of me. The words ring in my head, bringing panic to my chest.

"You, okay?" Jessica asks, noticing the way I freeze.

I try not to alarm her. "Hmm, not sure who it's from. I did meet a few people the other night."

Jessica beams, biting back a squeal.

"Easy, girl," I say with a short laugh. My heart thumps fast, feeling uneasy. I'm fully aware of who the flowers are from—*Dmitri*.

"Well, I'll leave you to your thoughts. I hope whoever sent these is very handsome. He has good taste." She turns, waving as she leaves for the day.

My eyes pursue her until she's out of sight, and then my gaze settles on the roses bleeding red all over my table. I have been fearing this today, waiting for a threat, ready for him to make his move. Only, I didn't expect it to come in the form of roses.

Bringing my face closer, the sweetness from the petals is beautiful, pervading everything and everywhere. Why do we women get so excited about roses? Is it a thoughtful gesture or just customary? Or perhaps it's the beauty of it? Whatever. I've never received roses as beautiful as these, only wishing they had been sent under different circumstances.

But I don't live in a fantasy, and these weren't sent because he's trying to romance me. It's a message. A message that he knows who and where I am and that he's coming for me.

After receiving the flowers, I think about staying in the office for the night, but I can't hide. I won't hide. Dmitri is from my world, and no matter how far I run, he'll find me. My mind stews on this on the ride home for the night.

"Goodnight, Elise." Alejandro shuts the door to the vehicle behind me, and I stand frozen in front of my building.

"Goodnight, Alejandro." I offer a quick smile, hiding the fear that's followed me all day. "I'll see you tomorrow morning." That last part comes out more as a wish than anything else.

I quickly unlock the building's front door, slipping in before Alejandro can drive off. Inside, I peer out the window to see if any shadows are hiding on the street corner. Slowly, I turn and head up the stairs to my apartment, not wanting to be caught in an elevator, unable to run.

On the top floor, I survey the hallway to make sure it's clear before quickly unlocking my front door and running inside. My sensor lights turn on as I lock the five deadbolts on the door and disable the alarm. At last ... Home offers a feeling of belonging, where my heart is. I can take off the dress, wear a pair of sweats and be myself.

But not tonight.

Tonight, I am hiding from a predator.

A heightened sense of fear arises, anticipating Dmitri and the danger he brings.

I walk further into my apartment, gun in hand. Right now, I'm so thankful for always leaving my doors open—bathroom, closets, rooms—as a precaution. It allows me to enter and walk through the place, ensuring I'm the only one here. I double-check the windows, ensure the bolts are locked, and check the front door another two times.

Finally, sensing I'm alone, I quickly shower, my ears sharp for the slightest noise. I decide to forgo ordering dinner and simply make a fresh cup of coffee. I sit in my reading chair in the corner of my room and attempt to read a book with my gun placed next to me on the reading table. It's midnight before I can turn in and seek sleep.

Tucking my feet into the warmth of my comforter, I check my nightstand, where there's another gun, checking the clip and making sure it's quickly accessible if needed. I leave the lamp on in the corner of the room and one in the living room to see if anyone decides to visit tonight. I lie quietly, unable to sleep despite tiredness, hypervigilant to every minuscule sound.

Time passes by. Lying awake, it's early morning. I'll have to get up in a few hours. Needing sleep, my eyes close, finally slipping into darkness.

In a deep sleep, my mind is clear. There's to be no dreaming tonight, my body lying way too rigid and heavy from the stress. Suddenly, I hear a noise.

My eyes flash wide, my head disoriented for a moment. It's still dark, the lights are all off. My pulse races. I quickly sit up and flick the switch to the lamp on my nightstand, also reaching to grab my gun. Then, his voice comes.

Chapter Fifteen

ELISE

"It's not in there." Dmitri's icy voice floats through the silence, startling me for a second, keeping me frozen, my hand still on the nightstand. I catch his figure through the corner of my eyes and swing my gaze across the room.

He's in my bedroom, sitting in the corner chair I use for reading, watching me. He seems calm, legs crossed, hands folded, eyes on me, and a weapon on the reading table next to the chair.

I'm too scared to talk, to say anything. My lips twitch, and I swallow a hard lump. I'm about to ask him to leave when he stands and comes to sit at the end of my bed next to my feet. Quickly, my legs curl to my chest in fear. I need to run, to scream, but he's too close and could kill me in a matter of minutes with his bare hands.

I could fight, but what use would that be?

"Elise, you've been a bad girl." His eyes are on me, a stern expression masking his face.

I exhale slowly. "Dmitri, I..."

He puts his hand up, telling me to be quiet.

"Elise, I'm going to ask you a few questions. I will not hesitate to kill you if you lie to me." He lifts his hands to show me how big and strong they are. Silently, I nod.

"Did you know who I was when we met in the bar?" His hazel eyes lock on me. I never imagined they could look so cruel. They send chills down my spine.

Softly, I answer, "Yes."

His eyebrows crease.

"I heard Andrei's brother was in town, and that brother was you." My voice is low. I am cautious with my responses, trying to answer his questions without further angering him.

My eyes remain on him.

"If you have dealings with my brother, why take an interest in me?"

"I wanted to know why you're back in New York City. Why now? Were you back to stop the deal from going through?"

"And did you find the answer to your question?" He places his hand next to my leg. I curl it away from him.

"No." I look him in his eyes, questioning him. "So, why are you back from Russia, Dmitri?"

He chuckles. "Sorry, baby. I can't tell you. Family business."

I don't press him because no more information will come anyway. But is something else happening in the Savin family and Coalition? I start to have doubts that Dmitri's purpose here is to stop my deal from going through—or at least, I hope it isn't.

"I presume you followed me to the bar. Our time in the bathroom, was that a bonus? Do you always sleep with your mark?" His eyebrow raises curiously.

Embarrassed but offended, I yell, "Fuck you!"

"You quickly let me between those thighs, practically begging me." He laughs and rubs my leg with his hand.

Slapping his hand away from me, I hiss, "Watch it, Dmitri. I'm not one of those little girls you're used to dealing with."

He stands, and his hands pin me to my bed in seconds. I scream, trying to push him off, but he's overpowering me. "Tell me, Elise. Do I need to watch my back since I've been sleeping with the enemy?" he says in an accusatory tone.

"I just wanted to watch you, nothing else. I didn't plan for any of this to happen." I give up, and my body relaxes under his weight.

He loosens his grip and stares for what seems like minutes, but it is only seconds.

Tears start to form in my eyes. "I didn't mean for this, Dmitri ..."

He silences me by putting his finger to my mouth.

My eyes are on him, and my vision gets blurred when tears flow down my cheeks.

Hovering his body over me, I'm oddly comforted by his closeness, even though I'm still pinned. Leaning down, he kisses my cheek where the tears are flowing.

"Blyad," he whispers as he continues to kiss my face, cleaning up my tears with his lips. He moves his lips to my neck, slowly shifting to my collarbone. His breath is warm against my body, his breathing deep and tense. Even with fear clouding my thoughts, every muscle in me reacts to him on top of me, his tongue touching me. A rush of heat spreads through my body.

So far, we've had a moment in a bathroom and an alleyway. Something about this moment in my bed seems different, more intimate. His hands work under my camisole, his fingers rubbing around my nipples. The tingling between my legs begins to torment me, and my panties grow wet.

My legs wrap around his waist. It catches him by surprise because he stops kissing me, and our eyes meet as though we are both thinking of our next move.

At this moment, desire clouds my thoughts. Letting out a deep sigh, I hide under his body.

He senses it, burying his face into my breast as he pulls my camisole up and over my head and my panties down my legs. He spreads my legs apart as his lips make their way down my belly, passing my belly button until he kisses my inner thighs. He sucks and bites my thigh, leaving a hickey, marking me. I let out a moan as my body reacts to his every touch.

He kisses me between my legs, spreads my folds apart with his fingers, and buries his tongue in me, licking and flicking slowly. "You taste delicious, Elise," he moans.

My hips rotate as I shove his face and tongue further inside me, hardening his pressure. My hand grabs the back of his head as I pant, a build-up of heat and energy creating a tingling pressure.

"Faster," I moan, begging his tongue to fuck me, but he knows the slow moves drive me wild.

"No," he replies. He continues to lick me slowly with his flattened tongue, in complete control of me, and I submit to him. With every touch of him, my body reacts, making me moan louder. It's a freeing experience to let go and enjoy what he's offering. Within minutes, my body shudders as I come on his face, screaming as I lift my hips, holding his mouth against my pussy by his hair.

I lie back, trying to catch my breath.

"One more night," I hear him say, removing his shirt. I want to touch his bulging muscles, so my finger runs along his chest, following the tattoo I noticed the first night in the bar.

"One more night." He starts to take off his pants.

"Yes!" I don't want to ruin the moment, not wanting to lose what we have right now.

He turns me over on all fours. "You've been a bad girl, Elise." He rubs a hand over my ass and spanks it hard. The loud smack echoes through the room.

"Dmitri!" I cry. A few more smacks, and my body burns up, aching for more.

"Bad girls get spankings, Elise." He smacks his hand across my ass again, twice. *Smack! Smack!*

"Dmitri!" I gasp, heat spreading from my ass to every other part of my body. His taking ownership of me brings a pleasurable rush. As a cartel boss, I've been ordering punishment for years. It's exciting to be the one receiving it for once.

"Shut up! This ass is mine, and it needs to be punished." His hand presses hard on my ass again, stinging. I feel the hurt across my bottom. *That's going to leave a bruise tomorrow.*

He leans down and bites my ass. "Ouch!" I whimper, and my voice gets interrupted by another loud smack and his low chuckling.

I've never felt this before, pleasure through pain. And I want more of it!

I'm still on all fours, and without warning, he enters me from behind. His right hand on my shoulder pulls me back, further into him, as his left hand comes around to the front and fingers my clit so I will stay wet for him.

Taking all of him is difficult at first, feeling the pain of every inch of him, but after a few thrusts, I enjoy every time he pulls out and shoves himself back inside me.

Dmitri locks my hair in his fingers before pulling my long, thick strands, not too hard, just enough to make me moan. He grips his other hand around my neck as he pulls me up into an upright position, his chest on my back as he thrusts, moving his hand back to my clit.

"Elise," Dmitri whispers in my ear.

"Dmitri." I'm moaning, feeling every bit of him. He feels so good.

"Elise, you are mine," he continues to whisper.

Confusion hits me, but I decide to stop thinking and just feel. Right now, my body wants to be his. But surprisingly, so does my heart. Everything about me, Elise Walsh, wants to be owned by Dmitri Savin. His claiming me brings warmth and comfort never felt before. The feeling rushes through me, making me orgasm. It's not an 'I just got fucked in the bathroom' orgasm, but an 'I want him to be my world' kind of satisfaction.

His cock swells, and he thrusts into me harder.

Pulling out of me, he grabs my hair, lowering my head to his cock.

"Open up, Elise." He rams his cock into my mouth, his depth hard to take at first, and he can tell I'm choking.

"Relax your jaw," he gently says to calm me. I do what he says and take every inch of him in my mouth, his moans letting me know how much he's enjoying it.

"That's it. I'm so proud of you." His movement gets faster as he pulls my head deeper into him until his juices rush down my throat, juices I swallow readily.

Dmitri has claimed me, and I want to claim him back. I want him to be mine as much as I'm his.

"Good girl, Elise." He rubs a little cum from the corner of my mouth. Leaning down, he whispers in my ear, repeating himself. "Good girl."

Waiting to be disappointed, I expect him to leave my apartment. But he doesn't. Instead, he lies next to me with his arms under his head. I curl up to him. My face hides in his neck, and my arm spreads across his chest. He pulls me further into his body. I don't know the last time I've stayed in bed like this with a man, truly soaking myself in his embrace.

This moment feels too good, too good to be true. It is, but I don't care right now, and in minutes, I close my eyes and enjoy the moment, hoping it never ends.

By the time I awake, he's gone.

Chapter Sixteen

DMITRI

Sitting at the end of the boardroom table, I look at each man across the room. "Gentlemen, do we have a deal?"

The man across from me rubs his chin and pauses. He stands and walks over to the window as though searching for something. The view from our business offices looks to Central Park, and he takes in the scenery.

"Dmitri, I hate that we've come to this moment. I wanted this business to become my family's legacy."

I stand and walk over to him. "And it will. Your family still owns a major share. The Savins know about family legacies. We want you and your sons to have that as well. We're just helping financially."

Turning to me, a look of defeat stretches over his face. "I'm left with no choice. But, if I'm going to have a partner, it might as well be brothers who understand what family is."

He reaches out his hand to me. "Deal!"

I excitedly place my hands in his, and everyone around the room begins to clap. We've just formed a significant partnership with a major technology company.

Concluding the meeting, I pause for a few minutes, enjoying the moment of closing my first major deal for our family since returning home. When all there is left in the room is Andrei and me, I glance at him. He's silent, his face blank, lips pressing into a fine line.

Usually, he sits at the head of the table, but when I walked into the room for the meeting, he was sitting next to our attorney. I slowly sat in his seat, guessing he was letting me take the lead since it was my deal. Not only will I become a Brigadier, but also, Andrei has named me Vice-President. Moving forward, all Savin companies, U.S. and Russia, will be operating under me. However, Andrei is still the Chief Executive Officer and is ultimately in charge.

He adjusts his tie as he stands and begins to exit. As he passes, he pauses. "Good job, Dmitri. Excellent work today." Then, he disappears into the elevator, leaving me alone.

It's been two weeks since my fight with him about Elise. Instead of addressing the issue further with him, I dived into my work.

Adam, our future Senator, called me to make a connection with Hawks Technology, which was searching for an investor. The team and I dove into their financial statements and made an offer before their bank could foreclose on their assets. A deal between us has closed today, expecting to make the Savin family businesses close to half a billion dollars in the next three years.

A celebration is in order, but tonight, I'm not thinking about the gentleman's club. Women, drinks, and cigars are far from my mind right now. I only want to savor this moment with the one woman I'm supposed to stay away from.

I left her apartment two weeks ago, telling myself that night was my last with Elise. I needed to stay away from her, but I was lying to myself. My body aches with a need for her.

Entering her apartment the next day, I installed cameras that would give me access to her entire apartment and the perimeter of her building. I wanted to know who Elise was. There was also the pleasant thought of seeing her every day, whether she wanted me to or not.

Watching Elise has become my obsession. Some women might find it creepy, but who cares? In the underground world, we do things differently. Elise understands that.

I sit nightly in my empty condo, waiting for her to come home from work. I like watching her throw on sweatpants, put her hair in a bun, and sit in her chair reading a book.

She's even gorgeous without her long hair flowing down her back and wearing a lovely dress. And the books she reads—even those that align with me—are all about financial and business strategy, like the ones I read. She's almost perfect in every way.

So, after closing my deal, I can't wait to come home and celebrate with Elise, even if she doesn't know it. Taking a sip of vodka, I turn on my laptop, watching her as she steps out of the shower. The drops of water falling off her body and the cool air hardening her nipples stir my dick.

Tonight, she skips putting on any clothing and climbs into bed naked, damp hair leaving water marks on her pillow. Her eyes are tired, but she's lost in thoughts, her lips pouting as she runs her finger over them as though her body is reacting to pictures playing in her mind.

I see her look directly into my camera for a quick second. But it happens all too fast. Did she even mean to do it?

The bed sheet slides down when she parts her legs, revealing her half-naked body glimmering like a gem under the moonlight. Her breasts form a perfect arch, their nipples erect. Moving her hand over them, her fingers graze the nipples, her body shaking, the bed sheet sliding lower.

As she moves her hands down between her legs, her body reacts to the sensation her fingers bring. She moves her hips slowly, matching her finger, circling her clit. I picture her lips close to my ear when she lets out a soft moan. Letting out a short gasp, she peels off the bed sheet and tosses it to the side. It makes me laugh, watching the frustration in that singular motion. Her needy pussy craves my cock in it.

"You wouldn't have to touch yourself if I were there with you, Elise," I mutter, reaching down to grab myself.

Seeing her body now, I watch the rising and falling of her chest and how she writhes and furiously moves her hand between her legs, slipping the fingers between her lips.

She inserts one into her pussy, moving up and down as she rides her hand. Her finger becomes two, moving faster and deeper, obviously getting close from how fast she bucks and throws herself up. Her hands move faster and her breasts shake to the rhythm of quickening breaths.

I feel a jolt between my legs when she cries out in a moan, "Oh, Dmitri!" Then, closing her legs, she keeps her hand trapped in between them as she rolls to the side, breathing softly. A few minutes pass before she changes position again, opening her legs and taking her hand out.

She takes her glistening fingers and tastes them. My tongue rubs my lips, imagining myself licking her lips.

After a moment of soft breathing and silence, she turns to her side, closes her eyes, and falls asleep.

Hearing her call my name has made me feel inside my pants and start stroking myself. I grunt and stroke the tip with my thumb, getting a few throbs from my rock-hard cock, pulling it free.

Sticky cum oozes from my tip. I rub it around and massage the length, using my other hand to play with the balls falling between my legs.

I think of Elise, my mind filled with the images of her touching herself. I imagine myself standing at the end of her bed, watching her while her eyes meet mine. My cock swells even more. The release satisfies me soon, cum dripping from my hand onto the floor in front of me.

After cleaning myself up, I sit and watch her soundly sleep for a few hours.

I miss my Elise. It's time to see her.

Chapter Seventeen

ELISE

"Goodnight, Alejandro." I jump out of the SUV, waving him off before putting in my code to unlock the front door. Looking behind me as I enter my apartment is now just a habit because, after that night, I no longer fear Dmitri. He proved he had no desire to end me. Instead, his only wish that night was to make me come as much as possible.

It's been two weeks since I saw him. However, gifts keep showing up in my mailbox. The first time, it was a heart-shaped diamond pendant, clearly from him, even though there was no card. But then came some high-heel shoes, a new espresso machine, and a few business books for my small library. The last gift received this morning came with a note, 'I'll see you soon.' The thought of being with Dmitri again makes my pussy throb.

Sometimes, I take the stairs to my apartment, but this morning, I chose to don the new high heels, so I push the elevator arrow and wait. I stand there reading emails on my phone when hands come around my face and over my mouth so suddenly that my heart jumps. I try to scream, but who would hear? Tears begin to run down my cheeks. This isn't the first time someone's grabbed me. It brings back frightening memories of my early days in the cartel.

"Quiet," comes a whisper in my ear. My body relaxes, thoroughly relieved.

That voice. The voice of the Russian man I've missed is the one I hear.

He releases his grip around my mouth but still has his hand around my neck. His other hand grabs the flesh of my upper arm, and he walks me through the hallway toward the emergency exit and out of the building.

"Dmitri! What are you doing here?" I wrestle with his hands. He lets me go.

"I've missed you." He steps closer, his fingers running through my hair. His eyes are deep and searching as if he expects a specific answer from me.

I rub my neck, and he looks concerned, asking, "What's wrong?"

"You scared me." My face disapproving of his tactics.

He touches it gently and kisses my forehead. "I'm sorry."

I know he means it, smiling at him with forgiveness.

"Come with me." He walks up to the sports car in the alleyway and opens the passenger door.

I hesitate, aware I should walk back into my building and straight to my apartment alone. But what's the fun in that? I'm curious about what he has planned.

He keeps his eyes on me the entire time, smiling as I make up my mind.

So, I get in the car. "Where are you taking me?"

"Do you trust me?" He laughs and closes the door. I look cautious when he jumps into the driver's seat.

"That's okay. You don't have to answer." He grabs my hand and kisses my fingers.

He turns the key, the engine revving. He reaches over to me and gently touches the top of my nipples with his hand, causing them to perk up. His hands move teasingly past my body as he grabs my seatbelt and buckles me in.

Without warning, Dmitri floors the pedal. The sports car takes off, sounding like thunder, and a spurt of adrenaline hits my body. "Dmitri!"

He looks over at me with the biggest grin, speeding through the streets of New York City, weaving in and out of traffic. I roll down my window and stick my hand out. Feeling the wind hit my fingers, I lean back against the headrest, closing my eyes and feeling the speed while the wind hits my face. My heartbeat races, and there's a tingle in my limbs. I haven't felt this free in a long time.

Hearing the engine slow, I open my eyes. We're in a secluded area near the water, looking at the most beautiful New York City skyline. This is why I moved to New York. The colors in the sky are almost magical.

Dmitri opens my door, and I step out, turning to take in the sights around me. "Dmitri, I love it. It's beautiful." My body gravitates toward the water, the cool air whispering like soothing voices.

"You're beautiful," he says softly, and he's looking at me, not the city.

Sighing, I avert my gaze. "The more we do this, the harder it will be at the end." I walk back to the car.

"I don't know how not to do this." He moves closer to me, closing the gap between us.

"I should never have walked into the bar that night," I say.

"I'm glad you did." His words make my mind a tangled mess.

"There's no happy ending to this story. We're both dead if Andrei and Liam find out about us." I put my hands on his chest, having missed touching him.

"We'll stay away from each other after tonight." His kiss fills me with emotion.

I pull away slightly. "We said that last time."

"We'll mean it this time," he mutters under his breath.

I give him a look. He's smirking, knowing we're lying to ourselves. But what's even scarier to me is wondering if he means it this time.

"So, after tonight, you'll take down the cameras?" My back leans against the hood of the car.

"You know about those?" He arches his eyebrows, an amused grin on his face.

"What, you think I don't have security in my apartment?"

"I disabled your security." So, he thinks ...

"You found my decoy cameras. Do I need to remind you I'm a cartel boss? I may know a thing or two." I remind him we're equals.

"You certainly do," he says with an impressed look.

My phone went off the minute Dmitri walked into my apartment to install the cameras. He cautiously went through my belongings, placing them back precisely where I had left them.

If it had been any other man, I would have had Diego break their knees with a bat. But it was Dmitri, and it was fun to play along. To be honest, I'd expected to hear from him sooner. So after two weeks, I decided to up the ante. And I was right. Touching myself was exactly what he needed to watch to bring himself to me.

He pauses. "You knew I was watching you?"

"Yes."

"You knew I was watching last night when you gave me a show." His face is flushed.

"Yes." I lean further back on the hood and spread my thighs open.

He cautiously stalks closer and places his body between my open legs. "Elise. You've been a bad, bad girl. And you must know what that means."

His dominant composure in front of me gets my body fired up, my pussy swelling as it tingles, and my panties moisten.

"I like being a bad girl," I whisper, winking.

Bending over me, he brushes his lips over my ear. "I know how to handle bad girls."

"Yeah?"

His hand moves up my neck, his fingers dipping into my hair. He pulls my head back by my hair and aggressively kisses my neck, puncturing my skin with his teeth. The pain excites me.

I moan.

With his other hand, he pulls down the top of my dress, exposing my bra before moving his mouth down to my erect nipples and nibbling on them. I grab the back of his head and push his mouth further into my breasts, wanting to feel every touch of his tongue.

Grabbing his shirt, I pull it over his head, baring his chest, then run my hands down his well-defined stomach muscles. My fingers twirl his chest hairs.

I kiss his muscles, and my tongue starts circling his nipple. When it grows erect, I flick it, and they only become harder.

My hands move down to his jeans, able to feel the stiffness of his cock, and my center gushes from the anticipation of him being inside me.

I unbuckle his belt and start to unzip his pants, his cock begging me to touch it. I grab it forcefully and begin stroking it, moving my hand up and down his shaft. His grunts let me know he likes it. Teasing him makes me feel as though I'm in control of him, that his cock is mine, and I'll do what I please with it.

He grabs my wrists with his hands and places them on the hood. He lifts my legs over his shoulders, pulls the side of my panties, and rips them off.

I moan at the excitement.

He's looking at me as though I'm his next meal, his eyes staring not just at my face but at my body and my curves, seeing every inch of me. My stomach aches for him.

He shifts my ass closer to him. Outlining my pussy with the tip of his cock, he moves up and down the wet slit without penetration, making me start to pant.

He drives his cock in me, thrusting in and out. Having him deep inside me, stretching me, is fulfilling. My pussy is warm and wet, and I squeeze my body around his cock. His grunts get louder, and my moans turn into screams.

My finger circles my clit. He looks down at me, watching me touch myself, and then he grabs my neck with his hand and squeezes it, my mouth opening wide in ecstasy.

An explosive wave of pleasure shakes my thighs as his cock swells and stretches me, coated with my dripping fluids, and his thrusts become more demanding and aggressive.

His body pounds on mine, his balls hitting my ass and sending a second round of liquids to flush down my thighs. He lets out a deep grunt and thrusts deeper, keeping his cock buried as far as it can go. I feel it swelling, and he erupts inside me, filling my pussy with his cum.

"Good boy," I growl with the tip of my tongue running against his cheek.

His head falls onto my neck as he softly kisses me.

We sit back on the hood, his arms still encircling me as the chilling air blows around us. We are spellbound by the beauty of the city lights and by the starry black sky sweeping over it.

His wet lips kiss my cold cheeks, bringing warmth to them. In his kiss, I sense he accepts me for all I am, not for the tough girl the cartel expects me to be. With Dmitri, I am free.

"I can't give this up. I won't let go of you, Elise. You belong to me. You're mine."

I move my lips to his. "I'm yours, Dmitri, only yours."

Chapter Eighteen

ELISE

What am I going to do? The more I think about the situation between Dmitri and me, the more confused I get.

My heart wants to be with him, but that isn't the reality of our current situation. I need time to think. My need for control is overwhelming, so I continue to dive into my work.

When Liam informed me I needed to accompany him to Mexico for a celebration for his father, I didn't argue. Tonight is Señor Martinez' birthday, so everyone in the cartel will be there to pay tribute and honor the man who makes us all rich.

I don't feel welcome in Mexico, aware deep down of not having a part there. I've only been there once before with Liam. Having a leadership role in the cartel, I must also pay tribute. So, I have agreed to go. In any case, I could use a break from New York City and hide from Dmitri for a few days. That should give me enough time to clear my head and think of a solution.

Señor Martinez is head of the Martinez Cartel. His reign started when he killed his older brother at fifteen and took over his father's business. He felt his brother was too weak for this life.

Liam is his eldest son, his pride and joy. So, he agreed when Liam wanted to come to the States to attend college. After graduation, Liam began setting up businesses on the East Coast so that they could extend cartel operations into legitimate businesses and further the Martinez name.

Liam's a visionary. His business strategies are planned out ten years in advance, ensuring profits for the long run, something I help with.

His brothers Erik and Elias, who run the Houston and California operations, only think about how much money they make now. They're not smart enough to project for the future. I already have plans to take over their operations whenever Liam is ready.

Therefore, the East Coast operations make up ninety percent of the cartel's legitimate money. We're an essential part of the cartel's operations to launder drug money in the U.S.

Señor Martinez runs the remainder of the money through Mexico with his nine lieutenants, who solely run the drug-producing operations. Being a lieutenant is a title of significance in the cartel. Carlos is Liam's lieutenant. If I were a man, I would be one too. But I'm not, so I'll never hold an official title in the cartel, no matter how much money I help them make.

Señor Martinez thinks my being a woman makes the cartel weak.

None of the cartel men's wives are allowed to work, and their daughters are usually married off through arrangements to solidify deals with other Mafia networks.

I never understood why Liam promoted me when I was not welcomed into the cartel, but I didn't argue. Liam is my boss and the one for whom I work. Señor Martinez is an unintended benefactor.

I don't visit Mexico, not able to trust the men there, the very men I work with. During my last trip there, one of the lieutenants threw me in a grave to show me what would happen if I crossed the cartel, a threat to bury me alive.

I was new to the cartel and cried in Liam's arms that night. That was all I could do. Holding me was all he could do as well. Liam may run the operations in the U.S. However, in Mexico, Señor Martinez is the boss, and he isn't going to punish one of his men over a silly girl. Instead, he laughed and said it was a joke. The traumatic nightmares of being thrown in a grave and having sand thrown over my body didn't seem so funny to me.

They don't care how loyal I am to Liam. I'm a white girl from the States, which makes me a threat because I'm not one of them.

I look up at Liam. My gaze is obstructed by the flight attendant who steps in between us.

"Can I get you something?" She asks Liam for his drink order, leaning over him so that he can see her boobs popping out of her buttoned blouse.

"Maybe you a little later," he replies, rubbing his fingers down her thighs.

He enjoys the perks of owning his own plane. I'm sure he'll be in the bathroom soon, his cock between her legs.

"I'll take a coffee." She doesn't seem to notice I'm sitting here or care to ask if I would like anything.

I don't like being ignored just because I'm not tall, rich, and handsome. Still, I'm the third in line on this plane, and cartel workers must respect that.

"Maybe you should be a little nicer, Elise," Liam scolds me.

"Maybe she should do her job, which is serving drinks, not fucking you." I roll my eyes and continue typing away on my laptop.

"Elise, when we get there, try and enjoy yourself. Drink some tequila and dance a little. Just stay away from the men," Liam warns me.

"While you boys enjoy Mexico, someone's got to do the real work." I let out a deep breath. When the men stay out late tonight enjoying their drinks and pretty ladies, I'll sneak off early and retreat to my work—more importantly, to my deal that's about to close.

Liam doesn't reply, quietly slipping to the back of the plane. After dropping off my coffee, I see the flight attendant walk his way until they disappear into the bathroom.

"You know he's right, Elise." Carlos leans over to me. "You need to enjoy life more. Why work so hard and make all this money if you aren't enjoying it? There are perks to being in the cartel. Take advantage of them."

Carlos enjoys the perks too much. He's overdosed multiple times, enough that we must keep naloxone on hand at the bar.

However, unlike Liam, Carlos understands what it's like not to grow up rich. He is one of the few people to whom I've talked about my past in Seattle. Like me, Carlos also grew up with a mom who liked bad men. His father is Señor Martinez' cousin, but his mom was a mistress who accidentally got pregnant with Carlos.

And I don't do all this for nothing. I do it for $147 million, to be exact, the sum held hidden in my offshore accounts. There's also a few million in cash concealed across New York and New Jersey in case of an emergency. I can thank the cartel for that. Dealing drugs is a lucrative cash business.

"We will be landing shortly," the captain announces over the speakers.

Here we go! Twenty-four hours, and I'm out of here; twenty-four fucking long hours. I fasten my seatbelt and prepare to land.

Chapter Nineteen

ELISE

Señor Martinez greets us in the foyer, walking over to Liam and kissing him on the cheek. Carlos walks up to his uncle, and they hug. "Glad to see you guys. You don't come home enough." He grabs two tequila glasses from the housekeeper and hands them over. They raise their glasses and sip.

I wait at the front door quietly. Señor Martinez suddenly notices I'm here, and his hospitable demeanor disappears. "You brought the girl." He gives Liam a look of disappointment.

"She's part of the cartel." Liam gives him a stern look.

"I guess we can find room for her." His voice is flat, and he doesn't bother speaking to me, only signaling his housekeeper to grab my bag.

"She'll stay in the pool house with Carlos and me." Liam grabs my bag from the housekeeper, and I follow him.

Señor Martinez doesn't respond, just walking off to give orders for his party tonight.

When we reach the pool house, I'm amazed at its size. The Martinez compound is a fortress. You would expect that from the king of the cartel himself, but even the pool house is more significant than any home I've ever lived in.

I'm happy to stay with the guys, wanting to be as far away from Señor Martinez as possible since this family has a reputation for cruelty. The drug business is complicated. Many newcomers try to make a name for themselves with equal brutality. Señor Martinez orders his men to hit back even harder. Nothing is off limits—killing, torture, corruption, or rape. And, in Mexico, Señor Martinez even runs the police, so there's no protection if he chooses to hurt me.

When I first joined the cartel, I only saw the side Liam operated. Under Liam's leadership, in the U.S., we do things differently. We're about making money and washing it through our businesses. But under Señor Martinez's leadership here in Mexico, there are no rules.

One day, Liam will control the cartel, and there will be change when that happens. Some of the lieutenants will retaliate, but it's a fight Liam and Carlos are willing to start.

"Elise, why don't you pick your bedroom first?" Liam points to the rooms and heads straight to the liquor cabinet. I don't plan to drink tonight and pass when he tries to offer me a glass. In an environment like this, it's best to stay sober and alert.

"I'll take the bedroom in the corner. I'm confident you two will be bringing guests home tonight." Laughing, we all retreat into our rooms.

In the bedroom, I throw my bag on the bed and start rifling through it, pulling out my dress for the party. Then, I slip into the bathroom to start getting ready.

I'm in a daze, my hands moving on autopilot, getting myself pretty for tonight. Still, my mind is again a thousand miles away, thinking about Dmitri. Would he like the way my hair is tonight, in a high pony with the ends fanned out? This way, I don't look too dull. Some light pink shimmery eyeshadow matches the flowers on my short, but not too revealing black dress. He's never seen me with my hair up, and I wonder—would he love it like this? I think he might as he loves to grab a fistful of hair, the high pony making that easier for him.

I blow out a breath.

"Elise, you ready?" Liam's bolstering voice echoes around the living room. He and Carlos have been shooting tequila since we arrived, and they're ready to start the party.

"Yes, I'm coming right down. Wait for me!" I look in the mirror one last time before walking out to meet them.

Liam and Carlos are very handsome with their chiseled bodies and darker complexions. Tonight, both are wearing black slacks and buttoned-down shirts, their cuffs rolled up to display the bulging muscles and veins on their forearms.

I walk through the crowd, watching the attendees enjoy salsa music and dancing the night away. The drinks and food are plentiful. I eat a few appetizers before settling for a cup of coffee, already noticing a lot of glances coming my way from both men and women.

The men hate me because Liam should have picked another man to help run the East Coast instead of selecting me. One day, Liam will be the head of the cartel, and the men want an opportunity to impress him—a chance that, in their minds, I have stolen from them.

The women, well, they think I mean more to Liam than I do. They want to be Liam's wife and the future queen of the cartel, a position they're afraid I might get. But they just don't understand our relationship, Liam and me. We're family, not lovers.

I stay out of the way, on the sidelines. Occasionally, Liam and Carlos check on me, and after I tell them I'm fine, they start mingling and flirting with the local ladies.

There's a big, beautiful flower garden on the compound. Liam's mother, now deceased from cancer, planted it, her garden acting as her sanctuary. The boys asked their father to keep it to honor her after her death.

So, I walk its length, admiring the various bright colors, a stark contrast to this fortress, this compound that feels like a prison surrounded by guards with guns. Liam once told me that his mother always tried to find the good in people or situations. Maybe this was her slice of heaven in a world built on evil and blood.

Honestly, I'm just trying to look busy to avoid people.

"Elise, you look lovely tonight." José, one of the lieutenants, approaches me.

"Gracias, Señor," I tell him, trying to avoid him by walking in the opposite direction. He's one of the lieutenants who laughed when I was thrown in the grave, begging for someone to help.

He follows me. "We don't see you in Mexico enough. Haven't been hiding from us, have you?"

"I don't have much time to travel." I try to answer while letting him know I'm not interested in a conversation.

He doesn't seem to get the hint, so I say, "Excuse me. I'm headed to the restroom." I catch a sinister grin forming on José's face, but don't pay it any attention. He's an asshole!

I feel an overwhelming urge to leave the party, but I'm not supposed to go anywhere without Liam or Carlos escorting me, so I look around for them and find them both half-drunk, dancing with beautiful women. Not wanting to ruin their fun, I flout the rules and head back to the pool house alone. My walk is pitch dark, and I need to watch my surroundings. The compound is so big that the pool house is on the opposite side of the property. Turning a corner, I run straight into José, who appears out of nowhere, a shadow peeling from the darkness.

"Elise, I wasn't done talking with you." He grabs my arm, and his fingers press into my skin.

"Well, I'm done with you. So, excuse me, I'm headed back." I attempt to shake his grip on me.

He laughs. "Not happening, Elise. You're coming with me." Grabbing my arm more forcefully, he puts his hand around my mouth.

I kick and pull away, but he's at least a foot taller and heavier. He's got his grasp on me, moving me through the yard and into Señor Martinez' home. He pushes me into the formal living room that sits unoccupied tonight. Once inside, he throws me on the couch, his deep laugh already crawling under my skin.

"Elise, you shouldn't have come." He leans over, sliding his tongue over my lips.

I gasp and push him away. "Get off me, you fucking bastard." I try to stand up, and he pushes me back on the couch.

"Elise, be a good girl and shut up." My fist hits his jaw. He rubs it lightly with a smirk.

Then, two more lieutenants walk into the room. "I see this is where the party is at," Petro says, walking over to the couch with a third guy I don't recognize.

"Fuck you." I try again to get off the couch, but José overpowers me.

"Let's see what Liam's been enjoying in America. Let's see how this puta earned her spot in the cartel." Petro stands over me, grabbing my face with his hand, trying to kiss me. I bite his lip, and he grunts, running his hand over the blood on his lip, then slapping my face with the same hand. I scream, but no one will hear me over the loud music playing outside.

José, still standing over me, starts to unbuckle his belt and zips down his pants. "Elise, show us what Liam likes." He spreads my legs around his hip. I try to fight, but Petro and the third guy stand over me, each grabbing my arms and hands to pin me down.

"Stop! Please," I'm pleading, crying. "Please don't do this."

"Oh, the puta is crying. Is this how things get done in America, by crying?" Petro laughs, kissing my face.

"Please, stop." I'm trying to hold my legs together.

"Fuck this bitch. Let's put her in her place before we each have fun with her," the third guy says, punching me in the chest.

I struggle, getting out from between José's hips, and turn on my stomach as I drop to the floor, trying to crawl away. The three men are laughing at me, while a foot is kicking me hard in the back and another in my side.

I'm crying, and it hurts so much. But I need to get away, so I keep on crawling.

They're still laughing, walking over to me, delivering one more kick to my side. The pain is unbearable, but I don't want them near me, so I keep crawling until I can't crawl anymore. "Please, stop," I whisper, too weakened to speak.

As the men take a quick break for a swig of tequila from the bottle, I quickly grab the small knife hidden in my boots. After opening the blade, another kick comes as Petro's foot hits the side of my back. Tightly gripping the knife, all my energy surges, driving the blade into his leg.

"Bitch!" he yells. Then, the sounds of a gun. *Pap-pap.* Petro falls at my side.

More gunshots fill the room. I'm unable to see what's happening, only hearing men speaking in Spanish as they fight around me. I lie too weak to move, then a hand curls around me, a familiar hand, and I look up to see Liam. His face is red, eyes flashing with fury.

"We're just having some fun. Come on," José begins to say when Liam points his gun at him, finger on the trigger. José raises his hands, pleading.

The bullet fizzes through the air and rips the man's left thigh. He falls back like a log, screaming and clutching his leg, now spurting bright arterial blood high into the air.

The third man lies on the floor, covered in blood from Carlo's beating. Scoffing, Liam smacks him with his fist. There's a loud snap; something has broken. Placing the barrel to the man's head, the gun goes off, and the man lies dead.

Liam walks over to the screaming José again, kicking his side. "Shut the fuck up already," he warns. José nods, his face covered with beads of sweat.

"I don't like men touching what belongs to me," Liam says, nostrils flaring.

José's lips quiver as he mutters an apology to Liam, the words barely audible between groans of pain.

I faintly hear Carlos warn Liam that it's time to leave.

"Elise, I got you." Liam lifts me into a cradle hold. It's the angriest I've ever seen him.

"Liam," I whisper because it hurts to talk.

"Let's go home." He carries me out of Señor Martinez's home and back to the pool house.

"How did you know where I was?" I cry, placing my head on his chest.

"I saw José talking to you, then you two disappeared. We came looking for you."

As I enter the pool house, I hear Carlos on the phone, ordering the plane to take off in an hour.

I feel weak from the kicks but also safe. Knowing Liam and Carlos are with me, I fade into an unconscious state until the plane lands, and Liam says, "We're home."

Chapter Twenty

DMITRI

Moscow, Russia, is an overpopulated city known for its unique architecture, the seat of government power, and the home of the Coalition's underworld.

Since returning to America, some low-life guys have tried to infiltrate our family business. The Savin brothers need to teach these scumbags a lesson, so I've come to make an example of them.

My brother Nikolai called the day after I spent the night with Elise, telling me to meet him in Moscow and help him take care of this scum and his crew. Usually, I would have passed, but dealing with Elise has me in the mood. This piece of shit is about to have a bad day.

"Motherfucker! Do you think you can mess with my family? You thought you would get away with it?" I kick the fucker in his bloody chest, almost killing him.

Nikolai got to him first, so by the time I show up in the basement, he's already spilling blood. He's breathing slowly but still wears a proud smirk.

The Russian tied up in front of me laughs. "Fuck you, Savin brothers."

Wrong answer! I hit him with my fists like a boxer getting ready for a match on the punching bag. Blow after blow with all my strength, fists against flesh and bone, the crunching sound cuts through the air.

Nikolai is laughing. "Damn, Dmitri. Who pissed you off today? I like it."

I keep punching the man, blood flying into the air. We don't need him. Nikolai cut him up earlier, so he's already spilled the necessary details of who he works for.

After that, Nikolai kept him alive in case I wanted part of the action. He was right, of course.

Beating this guy up with my fists is making me feel better.

The Colonel has sent a troop of his soldiers to find the man trying to infiltrate our business. Good, more assholes for me to beat later.

Nikolai finally steps in and waves his hand. "That's enough, Dmitri. We're wasting our time. He's a dead man already." The body is limp, his face smashed beyond recognition.

I grab a towel from one of the soldiers and wipe the man's blood off my fists. Meanwhile, Nikolai grabs a knife and tells the man, "May the devil fuck you in the ass in hell, motherfucker." Standing over him, my brother cuts his throat. In seconds, we have a dead man in front of us. I bet he didn't wake up thinking he would meet the man even the devil fears today.

Nikolai and I head upstairs to his office, sitting on the leather couch as his captain pours us vodka on the rocks. Nikolai raises his glass. "To my brother Dmitri. I have missed you here in Russia."

The taste of vodka lingers on my lips. "To Dad." I lift my glass to Nikolai.

He raises his in return. There's not a day we don't miss our father. Everything we do is to make him proud, even after he left us a decade ago.

I've missed spending time with my brother, Nikolai. When he's by my side, I feel free. He doesn't tell me to behave like Andrei, preferring when we don't. There are no rules with Nikolai. We do what we want when we want. We are the Bratva. It's our right to be who we want to be.

Whereas Andrei tries to make me more like him, confident but self-aware, Nikolai brings out the worst in me.

"What is it, Dmitri? What is on your mind? Something isn't right with you." He looks at me intensely.

"Nothing! Happy to be back."

He stares at me, sipping from his glass.

Nikolai Savin. He's the third eldest brother in the Savin family, two years younger than me. Growing up, Nikolai didn't care for the business side of things, setting a different path for himself. He became close to Colonel Lev when he was a child. He saw the Colonel with an army behind him, fearless, with many guns. He wanted to be just like the Colonel from a young age.

The Colonel respected our father, so he entertained Nikolai by letting him hang out at the warehouse with the soldiers. While most kids played with plastic or water guns, Nikolai was learning to shoot real ones.

While at the warehouse, the soldiers were torturing a man. Nikolai watched them. The men were laughing, then jokingly told him if he wanted to be the Colonel one day, he needed to be able to kill a man. Nikolai told them he wasn't scared to kill. So, they put a gun in his hand. That was Nikolai's first kill at eight years old.

The Colonel was so proud of Nikolai and his first kill that he asked my father if he could bring him to Russia to train, and my father agreed. So, when my brother wasn't in New York City, he was in Russia training to be a Coalition soldier.

When our father died, we were still teenagers. At sixteen, Nikolai solicited the Colonel's help to find the men who had slain our father. Then, those men and their families were tortured and killed by Nikolai himself. The Colonel was again proud of Nikolai, this time accelerating his training and rank in the Coalition Army.

When the Colonel had his first heart attack, the Coalition decided it was time for him to retire. Typically, they would have considered the Colonel's son to step up and take his place, but the Colonel and his wife had only born daughters. Hence, the Colonel recommended a marriage between Nikolai and his eldest daughter, asking the Coalition to consider Nikolai the new Colonel of the Coalition's Army.

Nikolai showed up on the day of the Coalition's meeting to decide the future of our army, telling them he would take the Colonel's position but would not agree to marriage as a wife would weaken him. He still does not intend to marry or bear children.

Out of respect for the Colonel, he did agree to arrange marriages for his daughters to higher-ranking soldiers. The Colonel, however, was disappointed in Nikolai's decision as he had always considered Nikolai, the son he'd never had. Marriage with his daughter would have made it official. However, the Colonel's loyalty was to Nikolai above his daughters, so he still nominated him for the position.

My brother Andrei, representing our family as a Brigadier, supported Nikolai. My father's best friend, Brigadier Valentin Volkov, did too. The older men in the Coalition feared Nikolai and any repercussions from arguing against him, so they all voted him for the position regardless of whether they thought he was the right person.

That was precisely how Nikolai ruled, through fear.

The final decision was on the Pakhan, who controls Nikolai and his army. So, with our uncle's approval, Nikolai became the youngest Colonel at age twenty-one. Everyone knew he was just getting started.

Now, my brother, the Colonel, sits across from me, asking what's happening in my life. If I tell him about Elise, he will torture her, and she'll be dead before I touched U.S. soil. I must keep her a secret from him for her safety.

My brother slaps his hand against his knee. "You know what? Let's celebrate you being home tonight and go to the club, have more vodka, and get some pussy." He stands up, laughing. Wanting him to stop inquiring about my mood, I quickly agree.

Tonight, the club is packed. As I walk through the VIP section toward the back, many businessmen and beautiful women greet me, welcoming me home.

On the plane here, I looked forward to returning to Russia with my people and the surroundings I'd called home for the past three years. But sitting in the leather chair, surrounded by the people I believe I have missed, only thoughts of Elise come to mind.

My men report that she's left on Liam's plane on a flight headed to Mexico. I figured she is taking care of cartel business and will be home in a few days. I stop lying to myself, saying I will stay away from her because it's clear I won't. My problem is I don't understand why I can't stop.

A bottle of vodka has been emptied into my cup as I sit here thinking, emotionally unstable and barely aware of my surroundings. My vision is blurred when someone I know approaches.

"Welcome home, Dmitri." Samantha sits on my lap, attired in the shortest white dress, her nipples all too visible through the tight fit. She's another woman with whom I would formerly have sprawled out in the backroom, her legs over my shoulders.

She giggles, her face lighting up, and she starts dancing to the music, grinding her ass against my cock.

I look over to my brother, Nikolai, who has two women sitting on his lap. He raises his eyebrows and winks at me. "Have a good time, Dmitri." He downs his glass of vodka before placing his hands all over the women.

"Get off me," I tell her, not intending to rekindle anything we had before I left. She grinds her ass harder on me.

I push her off. Almost falling over when I stand, I stagger to the men's restroom. Pulling my cock out of my pants, I hold myself up with my hand while taking a piss. My head is aching from drinking too much and from the loud pounding music.

Fumbling as I try to wash my hands, my pants are still unzipped when someone walks in.

Samantha is standing behind me, closing in on me, rubbing her hand over my cock. "I can help with that," she says, rolling her tongue.

"I don't need any help." I attempt to step away from her but fall back against the wall, too drunk to hold my balance.

Dropping to her knees, she pulls out my cock. My body is aching for release, but nothing about Samantha will satisfy me. I grab her hand to prevent her from touching me again.

My head shakes, sobering up. *Sorry, sweetheart, but this cock belongs to a woman named Elise.* I pull away and zip up my pants. "Not tonight." I walk out of the bathroom, leaving her.

Walking past the VIP section, I tell Nikolai I'm ready to leave. He tosses the redheads on his lap to the side, following me out of the club.

"Want a little action tonight?" Nikolai can tell I'm frustrated.

"What kind of action?" I'm not in the mood for another woman.

"My soldiers brought the informant's boss to the basement. They got all the information I need to take down their business, but I told them to leave him alive so you and I can have a late-night snack." Walking to his truck, he's glowing at the thought of another kill.

"I could go for a snack." I jump in, ready for more action. He knows me too well. This is exactly the kind of stimulation I need, not Samantha trying to seduce me.

Nikolai and I spend the next three hours slicing the man up with knives, cutting him the way a master butcher chops up a prize pig. After we fail to get any additional information from him, we finally put a bullet in his head. My brother and his men will attack his business and burn everyone alive tomorrow. My brother always brings out the evil in me, but I've had enough fun.

Covered in blood, I go straight to my room and shower. As soon as the water hits me, I start to feel relaxed and think about Elise. I stroke my cock and rub one out in the shower. I almost hear her moans when I spray cum all over the shower wall.

Feeling better, I head to Nikolai's office to get a drink before calling it a night. Before I enter the slightly opened door, a hushed voice comes.

"You are right. Something's wrong. He's not himself." It's Nikolai, talking on the phone. He pauses. "I had some blonde chick all over him tonight, but he didn't fuck her. When she pulled out his cock, he left." He's silent while the other person on the line talks.

I assume the other person is Andrei.

"Who's the girl? Do you want me to make her disappear?" There's a high pitch in his voice while saying those words—excitement and something more sinister.

"Elise Walsh. The smart bitch making the cartel a lot of money." He pauses again.

"It's not like Dmitri to get pussy whipped. You sure he's not getting her to turn on them and serve the Bratva?"

My heart skips, and I think about Elise and the prospect of having her in the family, accepted as one of us.

"If she's bad for business, then she needs to die. You almost sound a little jealous, Andrei. You two were working closely together," Nikolai jokes. Nikolai is the only one Andrei doesn't scold. I somehow wonder if even the powerful Andrei fears our brother.

"Let's keep an eye on him and the cartel woman. Give me the order, and they'll never find her body. See you in a few days." I hear him hang up.

I walk back to my room, the weight on my shoulders now doubled. It's time to head back to New York City and Elise.

Chapter Twenty-One

ELISE

The music in the club is loud enough to be obnoxious. The DJ instructs the crowd to raise their hands and jump, and they immediately start doing so. Coming tonight was a mistake. Before I can turn around to leave, a hot redhead approaches.

"Are we dancing tonight or killing someone?" Ivy walks up to me, swaying her hips to the music. Her almost see-through black dress leaves nothing to the imagination.

By now, all the men are glancing in our direction, making me uncomfortable. Ivy is always the hottest woman in the room. Her confidence exceeds her beauty, so she's inattentive to the men gawking at her. However, I prefer to be unnoticeable and hidden.

"Neither. I just needed a friend," I say, fidgeting with my hands.

She looks back at me curiously, knowing something is wrong.

"I'll follow you to the bathroom," she whispers, nodding toward the hallway. Walking toward the VIP bathroom with Ivy a few steps behind, I use my hair to try to hide my face from the room of men whose attention I don't want right now.

Once inside, pretending to fix my hair, I wait until the two girls admiring themselves in the mirror finish putting on their makeup. When they exit, Ivy locks the door. Then she turns to me. "What's wrong? Did something happen in Mexico?"

"Ivy!" My voice chokes up, and I try to take deep breaths. I want to let it all out, but it's hard to find the words, especially with Ivy's concerned eyes fixed on me. Right now, I feel vulnerable, a feeling I'm not used to. My mind flashes back to that experience in Mexico, shaking me.

I've been holding it in for the past week, but the seams begin to strain and rip. I sniffle and shut my eyes, burying my face in my hands as my shoulders start to shake.

"Elise. I've never seen you cry. It's scaring me. What's happened?" She steps closer to me and places her hand on my arm.

I swallow the lump in my throat and order her, "I need you to find everything you can on José Lopez, a lieutenant for the cartel."

Puzzlement crosses her face. "But don't you work for the cartel?"

"I need it to be an outsider. Something untraceable to me." If someone in the cartel heard me right now, they wouldn't think twice about putting a bullet in me.

I'm embarrassed to tell her about the three men and what they did to me. Since I've been home, I haven't been able to sleep. Whenever I close my eyes, I think of what happened in the Martinez formal room. I place my hand over my mouth.

But Ivy is the closest thing I have to a friend. She's had trauma in her past, and she will understand. So, I begin to tell her about what happened as I sob. She stands there listening to me, and her face softens, sadness in her eyes.

She embraces me when I'm done talking, comforting me in her arms. I remember it wasn't long ago when I did the same for her.

"Elise. José will pay for what he did. I promise." She holds my chin in her hands, looking at me with determination. "My face will be the last one he sees."

Knowing José will be a dead man soon brings me some comfort. I'm still frightened by the experience, but I won't let it consume me. José will die at Ivy's hands. When she marks a person, no one can stop her.

"Need some company tonight?" Pulling out her concealer, she pats some around my chin. She must have noticed the bruise I tried to cover up.

"Maybe next time." Tonight, I'm here on cartel business. "I have some men I need to meet with for work."

"You know, Elise, drug dealing is a messy business. It would be best if you worked on your exit strategy. Stay safe, my friend." She hugs me tightly, unlocks the door, and walks out.

I hear a few girls in the hallway complaining about the locked bathroom to Ivy. She snaps at them and continues to walk through the VIP section and out the backdoor.

I'm not okay, but my time with Ivy is a start. I wipe the tears from my eyes and freshen up before rejoining the crowd, moving on to cartel business.

I make my way to the back corner, due to be meeting some men here from a local street gang. Usually, I don't make appearances to men this low down the ranks, but one of them owes me a favor, and I've come to collect.

"Elise, slumming it, I see." The man in charge sits in the armchair. "Figured we'd get a visit from Diego tonight, not the one and only cartel woman."

"Why, did you miss me?" I ask, sitting in the chair next to him where one of his men stood so I could sit. No introductions are needed. They know who I am.

"Get rid of your company." I nod my head to the two women sitting on his lap. They assume I'm just another woman begging for his attention, so they ignore me and continue to dance with him.

"Go dance somewhere else." He smacks both on the ass, and they reluctantly get off, rolling their eyes at me. I blow them a kiss.

"Well, Elise?" He sits back, folding his hands.

"We'll give you your five-day extension with a ten-percent fee." It's back to business.

"Ten percent? Elise, hell no!" he shouts, moving closer to me.

"Then I'll send Diego at midnight to collect our money." I stand up.

He grabs my arm. "Wait, Elise. Ten percent?" I look at his hand on me. He knows he's made a mistake and quickly releases it.

"Sorry, Elise. Just caught me off guard." He pours more Cognac into his glass, then pours some into an empty glass and hands it to me. Of course, I won't drink it. I can never be too careful about people poisoning me in this business.

"You leave me no choice, Elise. Deal." He downs his glass before refilling it. "Like I said, slumming it tonight, Elise. I was expecting Diego."

When I started in the cartel, I wanted to learn all facets of the business and attended all cartel meetings. More importantly, I wanted to know the different players. But now I'm busy with the deal and too high ranking to make rounds with the local street gangs, so I usually send Diego to do my drug-dealing transactions.

I sit up closer to him to let me speak softly. "I need you to do something for me."

"Do something for you, or do something for the cartel?"

"Me." He nods and moves further into me. "I need you to find your cousin Amelia Clarke."

"Doesn't the cartel have its own accountants?" Of course, we do, but Amelia has secretly been acting as my personal accountant, something for which I pay her very well.

"As I said, this is for me and me only." I spot Dmitri at the bar, my heart stopping at the sight of him.

"I don't know where she is," he says, scanning the room. He's lying.

"Yes, you do. I know the FBI is looking for her, so she's underground. But I need her now and can't wait for her to resurface."

"I'll call her tomorrow and set it up. You're up to something, Elise. Be careful!" He tips his glass at me and drinks.

He's right. I am up to something, but that something is my business and my business only.

I place my hand on his shoulder to signal a thank you, and walk toward the bar. I try not to stare, but the man waiting for me looks devilishly handsome tonight, and I miss him.

Chapter Twenty-Two

DMITRI

My men have informed me Elise has come back from her trip. I promised to take the cameras out of her apartment, which I have done. Missing the constant visuals of her, I've since had my men start following her and report her every move. Is that worse than the cameras?

Maybe, but I can't take chances.

Now that Nikolai knows about her, he probably has someone watching her as well. Of course, he wouldn't do anything without Andrei's permission, but I'm not taking any risks. As long as my eyes are on her, I can keep her safe.

After Russia, I decided to stay away from her for a few days now that Andrei is watching me. It causes me an ache to know I'm so close to her and can't see her. My men report that her driver has dropped her off at Lux nightclub tonight. So, it's time to see my girl. I've taken a few precautions to hold her in my arms later this evening.

I walk up to the back door, security greeting me. "Welcome, Mr. Savin." They open the red ropes and let me walk through. I continue upstairs to VIP sure that's where she is. The club is busy tonight. I order a vodka on the rocks at the bar to help blend in, if that's possible.

When the manager notices me, he comes running up frantically.

"Dmitri! I didn't know you were coming tonight. Let me get you a VIP section."

His boss is my cousin, who also owns various nightclubs in Russia. A family business to launder money through, of course.

"No thanks. I'm not staying long. Just stopping by for a quick drink." I scan the room for her.

"Yes, sir. Let me know if you need anything." He nods and walks away, barking orders to some workers.

I find Elise in the back section upstairs, talking to some known local drug dealers. She must be taking care of cartel business tonight. She holds a drink but doesn't take a sip from it. *Smart girl.* I love watching her be a boss. The men around her seem scared, and she darts her eyes to the man in charge. I laugh, wondering what he said, obviously something she didn't like.

When she notices me, she excuses herself and starts heading my way.

I watch her move across the room. Something about how she walks, how her hips sway, makes my cock hard. She stands next to me a few minutes later and orders a drink from the bartender.

"You look beautiful tonight, baby." I can tell she likes that I call her baby because her face flushes red.

"Where have you been?" She takes a sip of her drink, the one she just watched the bartender pour. It's the first time I've seen her drink something other than coffee.

"Did you miss me?" I say, turning to her.

Biting her lower lip, her eyes soften.

"How was Mexico?" She slips into that expressionless, hard-to-read cartel woman.

"I don't want to talk about it." She turns her head away.

"You didn't bother to ask how I knew you were gone?"

"Don't have to. I noticed your men following me." I think she likes that I'm checking up on her, but I'm not entirely sure. She's so hard to read at times.

I lean over to her, whispering in her ear. "Can I kiss you? I missed those lips."

Her shoulders tense up. "Not here! We would be in so much trouble." She pulls away, looking around.

She's right. I forget about everyone else around whenever she is in proximity, getting so lost in her when she's this close to me.

"That's why I got us a room in the hotel across the street. Room 403. Meet you there in fifteen minutes." I slide the room key across the bar and walk away.

What happened in Mexico? That's something I'd like to know. I hope Liam's not trying something stupid. I clench my fist, thinking about her alone there with cartel men.

She slips the key into her fingers, and after a few minutes, she exits the club and heads across the street. Minutes after she unlocks the door, I enter. I've already ordered a bottle of wine for us ahead of time.

"Wine?" I walk over to the bucket and uncork the bottle.

"Not trying to poison me, are you, Mr. Savin?" She holds the glass up, looking at it.

I laugh, but there's a slight pinch in my chest. "Elise, if I wanted to kill you, I wouldn't have wasted my money on a hotel room." She chuckles in response and sips the wine.

Now that no one can see us, I lean over and kiss her lips. She kisses me back. I have missed her. I lean into her, putting her glass of wine down so I can kiss her harder.

"I've missed kissing you," I whisper, holding her close.

She buries her head in my chest and breathes slowly. "Me too," she says, her voice muffled by my body.

She glances up, and her eyes are glowing. There's sadness there. It makes me want to keep holding her and never let go. I tell her that, and she blushes.

"I'm fine," she says.

"I don't believe you." Something about her tonight is different; she's hiding something.

"Do you have a choice?"

I brush her cheek with the back of my hand. Grabbing her own hand, I lead her toward the bed. She stands still, waiting for my next move. For a woman in charge, she's very submissive to me and always lets me take the lead. I wouldn't want it any other way.

I walk up behind her and kiss her neck, collarbone, and shoulder with the softest kisses. She leans back into me with the slightest moan. This woman is a match that lights the fire in me.

Lifting her dress, I start to pull it over her body, and she quickly grabs my hand. "No!" She pulls away.

I'm confused. She was enjoying the moment. What just happened? "What's wrong?"

"I don't want you to see me tonight. Not like this." She tries to move away, but I hold her tight.

There's something wrong, just as I suspected. The look she gave me at the bar was not one of anger but of hurt.

"What's wrong?" I ask her again.

"Nothing." She's holding her dress, evidently not wanting me to see her naked. It doesn't make sense since she had no issue with me seeing her body before she left for Mexico. Quite the opposite.

"Elise, tell me." I hold her chin in my fingers and notice the bruise on her face. She did a good job hiding it with heavy makeup. I couldn't see it earlier in the dark club.

"Let me see." Tears start to flow down her cheeks. "Let me see," I whisper again softly.

My fingers touch her slightly, lifting her dress, immediately taking notice of the black spots on her body that weren't there before her trip. The more I see her covered in bruises, the angrier I become.

Tears continue to flow down her cheeks, and she won't look me in the eyes, fidgeting with her fingers and picking at her nail polish, something I've noticed she does when she's uncomfortable.

I suspect she's always holding a coffee cup precisely to hide that fact.

I pull her dress over her head regardless, kissing her, needing to see what it is that she conceals on her skin underneath the dress.

"Baby, what happened?" I comfort her and hold her in my arms.

I kiss her cheeks again. "Baby, you need to tell me what happened. Did they do this in Mexico?"

She nods.

"Liam?" I ask angrily.

"No," she quickly replies, then slowly replays the story of the three men who tried to rape her.

I can tell she's embarrassed and hurt by what happened, but something about her being open and honest with me now makes me care for her even more. I love seeing the boss side of Elise, but until now, I didn't grasp the other side of Elise's work, the side constantly exposed to the dangers of the drug-dealing cartel and how her being a woman heightens the dangers for her.

A fit of anger builds up inside me, wanting to unleash my wrath on the cartel. How dare they touch what's mine? Also, guilt consumes me. While those men were hurting her, I was busy getting drunk in a club with Nikolai. *I'm a fucking asshole!*

I will never let that happen again. From today forward, Elise will not leave my watch.

I'm going to kill those bastards, but not tonight. No, tonight, I need to be there for my Elise and show her how much I care about her, that this thing between us is not frivolous, not on my side.

Softly, I grab her face and kiss her lips. "Elise, you are mine and mine only. No one will hurt you again. But let me show you what you mean to me tonight."

Her eyes look into mine. She's more beautiful than ever. And she tells me exactly what I want to hear and means every word of it. "Dmitri, hold me."

Happy to oblige, I pull her into me and wrap my arms around her. We stand there hugging while she lets out a few more tears. With every sniffle, I find it harder to breathe and swallow the lump in my throat.

She looks up at me and kisses me, her hands moving to my chest as her fingers unbutton my shirt.

I begin to take my clothes off with her help. Her wandering eyes and the biting of her lower lip let me know she likes what she sees. If she only knew how much I want to belong to her and only her. "This is all yours, baby, and only yours."

She kisses my chest as I lean my head back and start to moan. Her hands and lips on me are driving me crazy, and my cock is hard for her. But I need to be gentle tonight. She's hurt, and I must show her that tonight is about her, not me. Some of my natural dominance must ease back, letting her tell me exactly what she wants and can take.

I move her toward the bed and lay her down, climbing over her, making sure not to touch where the bruises are on her body, avoiding further hurting her. Instead, I gently rub my hands up and down her small frame, continuing to caress her, wanting her to know I will never hurt her. She is safe with me.

I massage her nipples until they tighten. Lowering my mouth, I begin to suck them, lightly alternating between sucking and pinching.

I lick her neck before nibbling on her ears. "Elise. You are my every-thing," I whisper.

Slowly, I enter her one inch at a time, asking several times, "Is this okay?" She softly moans and smiles, and I take this as her response.

Our bodies move in one motion, up and down together, as we kiss, look into each other's eyes, and moan softly together. I grab a pillow and place it beneath her lower back to get a deeper penetration. Our bodies move, but I don't know for how long. Tonight is different. I don't want a quick release. Instead, I want to hold on to the beautiful woman and make love to her for as long as she lets me.

She whispers, "Dmitri, don't stop. I'm about to come."

"Come for me, baby. We'll finish at the same time." Unexpectedly, she pushes me back, rolling us both over and straddling me with my cock still thrusting in her. Her hands push off my chest, and her thighs glide up and down.

Her breasts bounce up and down with her body, begging me to touch them. I grab each one and squeeze them. She moves a little faster, letting me know she's teetering right on the edge, and I start thrusting deeper inside her, gripping her thighs with my hands.

"Dmitri!" Elise starts yelling, her chest lifting and her fingers fisting the sheets.

Her yelling my name is all I need to finish. As I come in her, I thrust harder and fill her with my cum. "Elise!"

She drops her body on top of me, and I hold her until we both stop shaking. She rolls over beside me. After wrapping her in a blanket, my arms curve around her and hold her tightly.

All those nights in the bar or club with my brothers drinking and enjoying women, I was searching for something. I didn't realize it until recently, not knowing it until this moment, lying here quietly with her in my arms. Yes, now I know that I've found what I have been looking for.

I have found solace in one person.

My Elise sees me not as a Savin or a Brigadier but as Dmitri, the man I am.

Chapter Twenty-Three

ELISE

I walk into my office smiling this morning, my cup of coffee already in hand. My night with Dmitri was amazing. I was so ashamed to let him see my bruised body, but how he held and comforted me confirms my suspicion that he may have genuine feelings for me as I do for him.

Last night wasn't about sex. It was so much more intimate than we've ever been. He comforted me, and I loved everything about the moment, never once feeling afraid or on edge despite the bruises. The more he penetrated me, the deeper he went, and the less I remembered that trauma.

"You seem happy this morning." Liam walks into my office a few minutes behind me, catching me by surprise.

"Just enjoying my cup of coffee," I say, smiling, still on a high from last night.

"You do love your coffee." He laughs. I roll my eyes at him.

"You're in early." Liam rarely shows up to the office before me unless something important is happening.

"Elise, are you okay after Mexico?" He sits across from my desk.

"Yes. I'm fine." I'm still embarrassed by the situation and that Liam had to see me like that.

"José will pay for what he did." I have no doubt Liam will take care of him if Ivy or Dmitri don't get to him first.

"I'm fine, Liam," I repeat. "I work for a cartel and know the challenges." My voice sounds matter of fact, detached, as if the words are true. In a way, yes, they are true but still, I'm concealing the real hurt of it. Sipping on my coffee, I really want to change the subject.

"You know we're family, Carlos and I." Liam is about to deliver some bad news. He always reminds me of our family before telling me something he knows will upset me.

"Always, Liam." I stop drinking my coffee and look at him curiously.

He sits up in his chair, leaning into me. Yup, he's about to deliver bad news. "We're pulling out of the port deal."

I almost spit out my coffee, caught off guard by how those words hammer down. "What! Why? We are about to close."

"My father doesn't want to deal with the Russians. The Italians are just collateral damage." He knows how much work I've put into making this deal happen.

I lean over my desk so he hears me loud and clear. "What about our import situation? I put together a great deal."

"Elise, you did well. It's not about your work. We're going to import through Boston instead. We made a better deal with the Irish." He says it as though he didn't just tank my career.

"Liam, this is my reputation on the line. I made promises to Andrei and Mr. Bianchi."

"I'm sorry, Elise. Things like this happen. The deal is dead." How long has he been plotting behind my back with the Irish? Something like Boston doesn't just come out of nowhere.

"This is about Houston, isn't it?" I knew something had happened in Houston when he made his comment at lunch.

"Elise, there's a rumor the Pakhan is dying."

"What?" I'm shaken by the news. "How did you hear this?"

"That's not important." This is big news in the underground world.

"What does the Pakhan's death have to do with my deal?" As I finish the question, I know the answer already.

"Andrei will be named the new Pakhan." The words escape me as I sit back in my chair. Wouldn't this be a good thing, to have a deal with the new Pakhan?

"It's not about Andrei. It's about the Savin brothers. We expect Andrei will announce Dmitri as Brigadier." Liam's chest rises. This move by the Coalition has him concerned.

"There will be three brothers sitting at the head of the Coalition. And, with Andrei's godfather, Brigadier Valentin Volkov, the Savins will control the entire Russian Bratva."

Now I know why Dmitri is back in town—to take his seat as the next Brigadier. When this happens, the Savins will be the most prominent family in organized crime.

"Remember, Elise. Cartel first," he reminds me before heading out of my office. Before he exits, he turns to me. "Elise, you'll lead the team tomorrow night to kill Dmitri Savin."

"Wait, what?" I stand up, chasing after him. "Why Dmitri? Andrei's the new Pakhan."

He grabs me and pins me against my office door. "Because you are sleeping with him."

My eyes widen with fear, a deep gasp escaping into the room.

Before I can respond, he scowls, adding, "I have plans for you, Elise. I don't need you being distracted by the enemy's dick. You've been a bad girl. Now take your punishment." He quickly releases me and heads to his office.

I stand there for a moment, taking deep breaths to calm myself and close my office door. I place my head against it, pounding my forehead into it.

Angry tears begin to fall down my face. I'm steaming. I place my face in my hands and scream. Evidently, loud enough that Jessica hears me.

"Elise, do you want some coffee?" She knocks softly on the door and asks this.

"Leave me alone!" I walk back over to my desk, punching the top of it, then screaming from the anger and pain shooting through my knuckles.

I feel as though I've been hit by a sledgehammer this morning. First, my deal is dead. I have spent months on it, and it is the perfect plan. A few minutes ago, all that work was stolen from me.

There will be no saving myself from this. My career has just ended. Any plans to leave the cartel are void. None of the underground families will ever trust me and work with me again. I'm stuck with the cartel. There's no escaping it.

Second, not only did my career just end, but now I will also be a target for the Italian Mob and Bratva. Mr. Bianchi and Andrei will not care that this was not my decision.

This whole thing was my plan. I made promises to them, promises I meant to keep, and promises I have now been ordered to break. I'll be running from both families for the rest of my life. I'm already in conflict with the cartel. Now, the Italians and Bratva will also come after me. If I ever lose Liam's protection, I'll be dead.

After kicking the desk twice with my foot, I lean against the wall and drop to the floor crying, face in my palms. Feeling nauseous, I grab my trash can and hurl up the contents of my guts into it. These past few days, I've felt unusually exhausted and queasy in my stomach. The stress from the situation in Mexico and this morning must be giving me an anxiety attack.

Dmitri Savin. What started as a recon mission has become the most exciting thing in my life, feeling a fire in my stomach and life in my heart when I'm with him. The man I'm supposed to stay away from is the one person I can't stop thinking about. And now, I'm supposed to hold a gun up to him and shoot him.

My phone vibrates, and I look down to see Alexis calling me. Immediately, I decline, then tap the back of my head against the wall. Liam and Carlos know about my sister. I have to protect her. If I choose Dmitri over the cartel, they will kill her. She's more important than anything, than myself even.

I know what I need to do. *Tomorrow, I will kill Dmitri Savin.*

Chapter Twenty-Four

DMITRI

After making sure Elise got home safely, I headed to Andrei's office feeling anxious and relieved. After last night, I'm certain it's time to tell him about my feelings for Elise.

His men part as I enter his office. "Dmitri! How was Russia?" My brother looks up at me from his desk, the corner of his lips twitching up toward a smile. I immediately recognize he's planning something, and it's big.

"Same as always—vodka, killing, and family." Sitting across from him, I decide to proceed with caution. It's time to confide in my older brother. "Well ..." I begin.

Right there, he cuts me off.

"Glad that you are here. I'm going to need your help dealing with the cartel." He leans back in his chair, folding his hands. My suspicion was correct. This is big.

"The Martinez Cartel?"

"Yes, we need to deal with Liam and his father." His face hardens, and his body tenses. He's also continuing with caution.

I try and break the tension. "I thought you had a deal with them that will be final in two weeks?"

"I thought so too, but my informants tell me Liam has been meeting with the Irish. There's been some rumbling about him taking over Boston."

"You think he's crossed you and Bianchi?" I'm surprised by the news. This move from Liam will cause a war between us, the cartel, and the Mob. The streets of New York and Jersey will drown in blood.

"I believe so." His crinkly eyes and pursed lips show so much disappointment. War is not how he wanted to start his reign as Pakhan.

"What about Elise Walsh?" I ask. "Do you think she knows?"

Elise surely can't know. This deal seems so important to her.

"It doesn't matter what she knows. She's part of the cartel. She dies with them." Andrei tries to read my reaction.

I try to keep a straight face, rubbing my hand across my body. His declaration feels like he just stabbed me in my chest.

"Andrei, I'm sure she doesn't know. She can't."

"It doesn't matter, Dmitri." He walks over to a board in his office.

"If Liam wants a war, he's getting one." Andrei unveils the contents of the board.

His whiteboard contains pictures of the Martinez Cartel leadership. At the head is Liam, followed by Carlos and Elise. Each photo contains pertinent information about the players, including their names, addresses, and hangouts.

While I was making love to Elise last night, my brother devised a plan to kill her.

Andrei lights up a cigar. "You ready to lead a war, new Brigadier?" He puffs his smoke in my face.

"If that's your order."

Elise looks so innocent in her picture. Yes, she's part of a cartel. She's even killed. But that's not the woman I'm in love with. There are so many layers to Elise that she doesn't let others see. But I see them.

I made promises to myself to protect Elise only hours ago, a promise I'm now being ordered to break.

He steps next to me. "Is there a reason why we shouldn't go to war?" I look at my brother to see the two of us staring at the same picture with hesitation.

He shakes his head, walking away from the board. I remain silent.

"Good. Nikolai lands in an hour." Then he's gone, leaving me alone, staring at Elise's picture.

Pulling my phone out of my pocket, I slowly press the call button.

"Hello," an angelic voice answers on the other side.

I continue to stare at her picture, hearing her short breaths on the line.

"Dmitri?" she asks.

My muscles tighten in my throat. I can't gather the words to tell her to run, crossed between my family and my Elise.

I hang up the phone, snatching her picture from the board before walking out.

Chapter Twenty-Five

DMITRI

"You ready for today?" I ask Andrei.

Standing next to my big brother, I feel like a little boy. It's my day, too, but being the new Pakhan is the highest honor my brother could've received. I'm proud of him. He's earned this.

Andrei speaks sternly. "We were born for this, brothers. We are Savins. Now let's show the men who we are and why the Savin name is legacy."

He's right. Before he died, our father had a plan to make us brothers the most powerful family in the Bratva. When he died, Andrei carried out that plan, and now look where we are.

As we ride the elevator to the basement of El Grande, where the Coalition's boardroom is located, the three Savin brothers embody strength, power, wealth, and, most importantly, family.

Nikolai has a smug smile as he places a clip in his gun. The meetings have a no-weapon rule, but since Nikolai is the Colonel, he and his soldiers guarding the meeting are exempt from that rule. It's comforting to know he's on our side.

The elevator door dings. Andrei is the first to walk out, Nikolai and I follow.

As we enter the boardroom, the seated men nod at our presence. Men come over to Nikolai to shake his hand and welcome him home. Where

Andrei and I are respected, Nikolai is feared, even among the men he's paid to protect.

Andrei sits at the front next to his godfather, Brigadier Valentin Volkov, whose smile flickers across his face. He must know about the announcement. He and Andrei are very close. He will support my brother and pledge his loyalty. The other men will follow him.

I sit with the remaining men of the Coalition while Nikolai walks around, making sure security has the place guarded. In an incident years ago, the men got too rowdy over the Savins. Since becoming Colonel, Nikolai has made sure Andrei's life will never be threatened again.

"Do you know what today's meeting is about, Dmitri?" Old man Smitty is well into his seventies and a friend of my father's. He is still a member of the Coalition but remains inactive due to his age. He and his wife couldn't have children, so his Coalition seat dies with him as he has no sons to pass it to.

"I think the Pakhan is making an announcement," I tell him in a hushed voice.

"It's good to see you, Savin boys. You all look like your father. No Anton or Alexi today?" He studies the room.

"No, they're working in Europe." Our twin brothers hate New York and try to stay away as much as possible.

"I hear Andrei is expecting his first child. Please pass my congratulations to him if I don't get to speak to him today."

"I will. Thank you."

Old man Smitty and his wife would check on us often right after our father died. They did it because they loved our father and not because they wanted something from us. I will always be grateful to him and his wife for the kind gestures they showed to my mother and our family.

"When do you plan on settling down with a lucky lady?" He knows the reputations of me and my brothers with the ladies.

"When I find a woman as beautiful as your wife." I pat him on the knee.

He laughs and turns to stand when the Pakhan enters, showing his respect for our leader.

Our uncle sits in the middle of the table with the five Brigadiers and my brother Nikolai next to him. As the Colonel and leader of the Coalition's army, Nikolai gets a seat next to the Pakhan alongside the Brigadiers.

We sit back in our chairs when the Pakhan begins to talk. He looks nervous. It's not an easy task to walk away from being Pakhan. As Pakhan, you are the most important man in the Russian Bratva. All the men in this room and the men working for us serve the Coalition, and the Pakhan controls it.

"I know you are all eager to know why I gathered you here for this special meeting." The Pakhan stands to show how important this announcement is. "I'm sick. I don't have much longer to live." The audience gasps, now realizing a new Pakhan will be named today.

"As you know, I have no son to pass my seat to. However, God did bless me with family." Everyone turns to Andrei, the natural choice. "Today, I am resigning my seat and passing Pakhan duties to my eldest nephew, a man who lives for and loves the Coalition. A man whose father sat in the seat in which he sits today, a man raised to be the future Pakhan. Today, I will pass this ring to my nephew, Andrei Savin."

The Pakhan takes off his ring and passes it to Andrei. Since the beginning of the Coalition, it has been passed on to new Pakhans as a signal of being our ruler.

Andrei accepts the ring and his new role as Pakhan.

I stand, clapping heartily for my brother. The men around the room join me and clap as well. Old man Smitty is smiling. I can tell he is proud of my brother, too.

"What about Andrei's brigadier seat?" a man asks.

Valentin stands, addressing him. "The brigadier seat belongs to the Savin family. They are Coalition legacy, so Dmitri will now hold the seat and the Brigadier title." The men around the room nod, showing support, but the man does not.

"That's three Savin brothers at the head of the table. No family has ever held that much power in the Coalition," the man voices and stands, trying to get others to agree with him. I see others wondering if they should stand as well.

Before they can do so, my brother Nikolai rises and says, "Are you challenging the Pakhan on his decision?" The room falls silent as he speaks.

"No, Colonel. I was merely saying this hasn't been done before." The man sits back in his chair, no longer urging any others to join him.

"If you aren't challenging the Pakhan's decision, then your statement is not warranted."

Men are allowed to discuss the Pakhan's decisions and even challenge them. But they should remember that to challenge often means death. Nikolai is flexing his muscles, knowing no one will challenge the new Pakhan. To challenge Andrei is to challenge Nikolai.

A man yells from the back, "Cheers to the new Pakhan and Brigadier. To the Savin brothers!" He raises his glass, and the men around the room follow.

The new Pakhan, Andrei, ends the meeting.

I watch Nikolai walking toward the man who questioned our uncle's decision. The man notices and quickly starts to walk out of the boardroom. Nikolai steps a few steps behind him as they leave the basement.

It's against the rules to kill another Coalition man, but that won't stop Nikolai from beating him, showing the other men that questioning Andrei will not be tolerated. It's Nikolai's way of placing fear in the men before they decide to question his authority.

This poor man will get that harsh lesson tonight.

I walk around the room shaking hands, accepting the many congratulations the men are greeting me with. The man was right, though. This is the first time three Savin brothers have held leadership positions in the Coalition. Tonight, we have become the most important family in the Russian world.

Our father would be so proud.

Chapter Twenty-Six

DMITRI

"I have my boys home. I'm so excited to see you all." The voice is sweet and welcoming.

Our mother walks into the living room, hugging us and kissing Cora. "I can't wait for my first grandbaby." She rubs Cora's pregnant belly, a bright beam on her face.

"So, what did we decide to name him?" Our mother asks Andrei.

"Sasha Savin," he says proudly. A slight tear drops from Cora's eye. Andrei rubs it away with the light touch of his finger and kisses her on the cheeks.

"That's a great name for our future Pakhan," our mother says proudly. Nikolai and I nod in agreement.

When our father died a decade ago, our mother moved out of El Grande to our family home in upstate New York. Nowadays, she only comes to the city for social events and occasional shopping trips.

She was a Brigadier's wife and a Russian princess as the Pakhan's sister. Her and my father's marriage was arranged between the Pakhan family and Savins. She understands our life. She grew up in it.

Our mother and Cora understand each other; their paths are identical. Cora also grew up in the Coalition with the same fate, having been promised to Andrei as a debt payment as a child. But the arrangement didn't matter to them. They had been in love since they were both in kindergarten, so Cora had always belonged to him.

Only Coalition men were allowed to attend yesterday's meeting. Our mother has planned a family dinner to celebrate this momentous occasion. She also wants to see Nikolai, reminding him he doesn't come home as often as she would like.

"Nikolai, how long are you in town for?" Mother turns her attention to him.

"I'll be in town for a while." Nikolai doesn't stay in the same place for more than a few weeks because of his duties leading the Army.

"I'm happy to hear that. Maybe I'll come to the city to spend some time with you." She pats him on the arm.

"Maybe." Nikolai barely answers her.

Our mother won't push any further. Even she is sometimes frightened by her own son. Of the five brothers, Nikolai is the least close to our mother because he spent so much time training in Russia that he didn't bond with her growing up.

Saving my brother from having to indulge her any longer, I ask, "What's for dinner tonight?"

"Pirozhki and stroganoff with lamb." She starts heading to the dining room, and we all follow.

My father was a busy man, but he tried to make it home for dinner as much as he could. We grew up sitting around the table for family dinners. Time together every night is one of the reasons why we are a close family. It's the one thing I missed as we all began to get older and live our lives.

We gather around the formal dining table, Mother sitting at the end where she used to sit when my father was still alive. On the day of our father's funeral, however, Andrei started sitting in his seat, showing he was the new leader of our family.

The housekeeper comes in and pours red wine into the glasses around the table. I'm sure it's something expensive our mother has picked out personally from the wine cellar. After our father's death, she spent much more time in the cellar getting acquainted with various wines. We indulged her as we knew she had loved our father deeply and was taking his death hard.

"Today, you boys continue the Savin legacy. Three brothers are sitting at the head of the Coalition table. I am so proud of you all." She raises her glass. We follow and raise ours before taking a sip. Tonight, we celebrate, but tomorrow, we start a war with the cartel.

Then, after the cartel, another new war will begin. Challenges are inevitable when a family like ours holds too much power in our world.

"Cora, how does it feel to be a Pakhan's wife now?" Our mother takes pride in being a Brigadier's wife and now, the Pakhan's mother. She's always dictating to Cora to be like her.

"I'm proud of Andrei." She leans over and kisses him. It makes me think of Elise, wondering if Cora and Elise would be friends. They are complete opposites.

Cora is the perfect trophy wife for Andrei, being humble and caring, spending a lot of her time doing charity work on behalf of the Savin family, and occasionally writing romance novels. She's an author second to being Andrei's wife.

Elise is different, ambitious. She's killed men, and men have tried to kill her. She's not the wife you come home to for support at the end of the day. She supports her man by closing deals and making money. And I mean billions.

The housekeepers start to bring dinner to the table as we sit and chat, feasting on the delicious food our mother had the staff prepare tonight. None of us has grown up cooking or cleaning. We have always had staff since our childhood. It's the privilege of being a Savin child. Cora's son, the future Pakhan, will grow up with that same privilege.

"So, Dmitri and Nikolai, when will you two start settling down with a young lady and maybe have children?" Our mother asks, posing the same question every time we see her. Now that I'm the new Brigadier, my mother and Andrei's pressure to take a wife and have a son will increase.

Nikolai growls. He's made it very clear he won't take a wife or have children. He doesn't entertain our mother with an answer.

It's different for me. I've always planned to take a wife one day but have never met a woman to whom I want to give my last name. But now, thinking about it and imagining myself having a wife, Elise is the woman I see next to me. Yes, I would make Elise Walsh a Savin if the circumstances were different. If it weren't for Andrei's orders to kill her in this upcoming war.

I hear my mother speaking. "Sorry, what?" I look at her.

"Now that you are back in New York City, have you been out on dates? There's a lot of beautiful young Russian women in the city." I'm sure she has a few she wants to set me up with.

My brothers are glaring at me, clearly knowing about Elise and me, even if I won't admit it. "I've been busy working, Mother. I haven't had much time for dating. We just closed a major deal recently."

"I heard. I'm proud of you, son." Our mother has always shown how proud she is of each of us and what we accomplish. "Well, make sure you have some fun as well because ..."

Our mother never gets to finish her statement as a bullet smash through the window to embed itself in the wall behind me. The sound of glass shattering ripples through the room, followed by screams.

Chapter Twenty-Seven

ELISE

Acres of trees and beautiful gardens surround the Savin mansion. After disabling the alarms and circumventing the tripwires, the men and I infiltrated the compound. We are standing in the yard unnoticed, ready to attack.

"Waiting for your orders, Elise," Diego whispers to me.

I grab the binoculars to get a better view of the house. A few armed men stroll its perimeter. I spot the captain giving orders to the soldiers, who nod and disperse into various areas. The outside of the house is incredibly quiet, although movement comes from the inside.

My gaze shifts toward the window.

Dmitri and his family sit enjoying a family dinner. Around the table are the three Savin brothers, Cora, and an older woman. I guess she's their mother. Like any other family, they sit, eat, talk, laugh, and drink copious wine. I imagine this is something they often do, as it seems they are all content in this scene.

For me, there was never any formal dining room to sit around or family dinners to enjoy when growing up. Most of my dinners I ate alone while my mother was out on dates. Even today, whenever I want comfort food, I make a grilled cheese sandwich.

My mind pictures how sitting next to Dmitri and being part of family dinners would be. The thought gives me a warm feeling and a smile appears on my face.

"Elise, are you ready?" Diego nudges me, pulling me out of my imagination and back to reality.

Glancing at Dmitri again, I decide it's time to do what I must do. The more I watch him, the more this decision weighs heavily on my heart.

"Sniper, take the shot," I say, ordering the man to my right.

I can't do this. I can't live without Dmitri in my life. "Wait!" I quickly tell the sniper, but it's too late. Within seconds, he pulls the trigger.

My interruption makes the sniper jerk and the bullet misses Dmitri, hitting the wall behind him.

"What the fuck, Elise?" Diego scowls at me.

"I thought I saw something. Let's move forward." Leaving the snipers in place, I lead the men around the yard toward the house. My hands wave in the air, signaling the men to flank. By now, security and Coalition soldiers have started to return gunfire. Patting my bulletproof vest, I continue toward the house, undaunted. As gunfire rains around me, I take cover behind a tree while the cartel men continue to advance.

Three of them take a bullet and fall, dead on the ground only a few feet from me, fast bleeding out. It's no surprise. I have been expecting casualties; aware this war would be a hard fight.

Diego never leaves my side, probably at Liam's orders. I peek around the tree toward the window from which Dmitri and his brothers return fire, aiming at the men to my left. I have no sight of the women; they must be hiding. In any case, I have no intentions of killing a pregnant woman, happy to see Cora taking cover.

After reloading, I think of my sister and what Liam will do to her if I fail my mission. I must choose my sister before myself. My arm extends out past the tree trunk, gun in hand, patiently waiting for Dmitri to come up from the table to fire a round of shots. Still hesitating, after several minutes, I haven't pulled the trigger.

"Elise, take the shot," Diego growls.

I think again about my sister, determined to protect her. "Patience, Diego." I patiently wait, aiming toward the window.

Dmitri stands, walking toward the side of the room, in full view, fully exposed. With my hands shaking, I pull the trigger. I must have hit him because he grabs his shoulder and falls, not coming up again.

Leaning my head against the tree, I let out a soft cry.

And it hits me. I have just slain the man I love.

I press my hand over my mouth, so the men don't hear me cry. But it doesn't matter. When I look over, Diego is watching me. He knows I'm vulnerable and will use it against me.

The once quiet air is now rocked by continuous roars of gunfire. "Helicopters are five minutes out," the voice crackles on the radio. Nikolai has called for backup.

Half the cartel's men are dead on the ground, and we are in no position to continue the fight, so I order the men to retreat, wiping my tears with my arm and preparing to move out. "Snipers, stay in place until the men and I are off the compound," I order over the radio.

"Diego, I'll cover while you lead the men out," I command. Diego doesn't leave my side.

"I'm right behind you," I assure him. He returns fire on Russian soldiers as the men retreat past the snipers. I stay hidden behind the tree and kill two enemy soldiers as my men start disappearing into the trees.

Dmitri is dead. It's now time for me to return to Liam and face judgment from the cartel for my actions. I turn to head in the opposite direction of the house when I meet the end of a gun barrel. My heart stops.

"Look what I got here," he smirks. The captain stands in front of me with a gun aimed at the middle of my forehead. My men turn to head back for me, and I signal for them not to. It's too dangerous. Soldiers are on their way. They need to leave. Diego is hesitant, and my head shakes again. He reluctantly orders the men to retreat, and they disappear into the dark.

The captain grabs my arm and pulls me to the house where cartel and Russian men lie sprawled out along the yard. All covered in crimson. Dead.

The captain is Nikolai's right-hand man and best friend. Nothing about him is kind, and he aggressively pulls me through the house until I'm standing in front of the Savin brothers.

"Colonel, here's the bitch leading the cartel. She pulled the trigger, shooting Dmitri." He throws me across the room, and I fall to the ground, catching myself with my hands.

Dmitri is standing there, clutching his shoulder, his hands stained with blood.

He's alive! I let out a breath of relief, crawl up from my knees, and stand before the Savin brothers. Their lips tighten, their faces hardening as my body begins to shake. Standing in front of me are three ruthless Bratva bosses with whom I've just started a war, each pointing a gun at me. My punishment will be cruel.

Dmitri walks toward me and grabs my neck, squeezing it to the point where I can't breathe, the stickiness of his blood rubbing against my skin.

"Elise, you've been a bad girl," Dmitri says before shoving me hard against the wall.

Chapter Twenty-Eight

DMITRI

The woman I love is standing before me, dressed for war. This is a different side of Elise, the cartel side. Her tight, black outfit with knives and holsters around her thighs—where I presume she holds her handguns—makes my cock ache.

I cringe when the captain throws her on the ground like a rag doll. Haven't I already made it clear I don't like men touching her?

Andrei grabs me, and I pause, remembering the situation at hand.

Here, I have spent the day dreading the war with the cartel which we have planned to begin tomorrow, not thinking it would be Elise who'd come for me first. Not many women would start a fight with the Savin brothers. I might have been impressed if not for the fact she shot me.

But Liam gave the orders. The Elise I held the other night wouldn't shoot me. When she looked at me after coming hard on my cock, her eyes told me she loved me.

She stands in front of my brothers and me, expressionless, ready for a fight. Her eyes dart between the three of us, and she notices our guns. A woman like Elise is smart enough to know she will be punished in the worst way. Regardless of her orders, she has betrayed me, and I feel hurt by her. I've never felt hurt by a woman before, and it doesn't sit right, making me furious.

My anger consumes me. "Elise, you've been a bad girl." I grab her, slamming her against the wall. "You fucking shot me!" Holding my grip around her neck, I push her against the wall again, her head hitting it, and she lets out a cry.

"Dmitri!" She starts to sob.

I'm not sure if she's sorry or crying because she's scared. It doesn't matter. What matters is that she took the first shot, and now any chances of trying to save her from my brothers are lost.

The room is still. The sound of me releasing the safety on my gun fills the air. Her eyes widen, and her chest sinks in when she hears it.

I slowly lift the gun and place the barrel to her head. She closes her eyes as the tears continue to fall down her cheeks.

Her mouth quivering, she murmurs, "I'm sorry!"

"I loved you." My words of affection sound harsh, surprising myself by saying those words. I've never said them or even felt them before meeting Elise.

Her eyes open as she looks up at me, our gazes meeting. "I love you, too."

I know she means it. If only things were different. I wish Elise and I had a future, but we don't. She's cartel. I'm Bratva. That's the reality of our situation.

I stand there for a moment, my brothers' eyes on me, and I know what they expect me to do. I'm just not sure I can, hesitating.

"Pull the trigger. If you're not dead, I am!" she yells. "Pull it, dammit!"

She really orders me as if I am one of her men, demanding I act as my role requires? It is almost too much to contemplate, but she sees the seriousness of my role, demanding I keep it, that I stay true to it, even if it means her brains, blood, and skull spatter the room.

She sniffles and closes her eyes as if making peace with her fate. At least that's what she wants us to think, but her heart is beating fast, those beautiful long fingers fidgeting. She's scared.

I stand there for what feels like minutes. Crying sounds from Cora and my mother fill the room. They know what I'm about to do. Everyone stands still, waiting.

Waiting for me to execute Elise.

I can choose to kill her or decide to let her go and suffer the consequences. Before Elise came along, I wouldn't have questioned myself, seeing no problem killing anyone whose last name wasn't Savin. But I've done this to myself.

I've chosen Elise as mine instead of walking away. The woman I promised to protect in room 403 and also vowed to slay on Andrei's orders stands before me, awaiting her fate.

My eyes don't leave her, the thumping in my chest loudly filling my ears.

Letting out a deep sigh, I pull the trigger.

She gasps, and her eyes widen. The clip is empty. I ran out of bullets before the shooting stopped. I take a deep breath, lowering the gun, taking a few steps back.

Andrei had stepped forward when I put the gun to her head. Relief now crosses his face.

Even when I confessed my love for Elise, he had only sympathy for her, none for me. It's ironic, given the fact that he was the one who ordered me to kill her.

Would he have let me end her life?

It doesn't matter because I've decided her fate.

I look at Elise, no longer the expressionless woman hiding behind the cartel name. The woman in front of me seems pained and remorseful. Her eyes are saddened, and the tears continue to cascade. Her skin is paler than before as her chest rises from her hardened breaths.

Even when I want to kill her, Elise's lips make me want to kiss them, and her body makes my cock press against my pants.

There's only one choice for me to make. "Run!"

"What?" She's surprised.

"I don't think so." Nikolai steps to us and holds his gun up to Elise.

I grit my teeth, stepping in between Nikolai and her. "This is between Elise and me."

"No, it's not. She shot at our family. She's cartel. She's a dead woman." As he grips the gun tighter, Andrei steps up to Nikolai with his finger on the trigger.

"Put the gun down, Colonel." Nikolai doesn't budge. "That's an order," Andrei commands.

Nikolai smirks and puts down his weapon, cursing fiercely.

"Run and hide, Elise. If I find you, I will not hesitate to put a bullet in you. Run!" I warn her.

Nikolai will not let this go. I don't trust my brother, and right now, I can't trust Elise.

"Dmitri." She steps toward me, raising her hands to touch me.

I need her to leave, stepping further back from her and turning my back to her before clutching my shoulder. The adrenaline shielded the pain of her gunshot. Suddenly dizzy and unable to feel my arm, I drop to the ground.

I'm disoriented, watching Elise scream, "Dmitri!" She moves toward me until Andrei steps in front of her.

"It's time for you to go." She peeks around him at me, shaking her head. "Now, Elise," Andrei scowls.

Elise backs out of the room and disappears.

I know I've disappointed my brothers, but I don't care. The one thing I care about in the world is a woman who is now crying and running in the opposite direction. She's hurt. I'm hurt. Tonight, we both lost something. We lost each other.

I close my eyes, and there's nothing but darkness.

Chapter Twenty-Nine

ELISE

EIGHT MONTHS LATER

The waves of the ocean wash calmness over me, my soul needing the sea after I left New York, my job, and my lover, Dmitri. I'd worked hard, giving the cartel most days of my life to be successful, and now, somehow, I'm here—as far from New York as I can be—in San Diego.

I left that night fearing for my life, packed up, got in the car, and drove as far as the road could take me, the I-80 bringing me here.

I hid for months in fear that someone was looking for me and would find me, but when no one came, I decided to make this my new home.

My years in the cartel have made me more money than I can possibly use in my lifetime. One call to my accountant, Amelia, to access my foreign accounts, and I find I can easily buy this two-bedroom condo looking out onto Mission Beach. Every day, I look out this window at the waves and think about my life, missing New York, missing my job—and missing Dmitri.

But I can't go back. It's not just about me anymore. I have another to protect. I hear a faint cry behind me, smiling as I see the most beautiful hazel eyes looking back at me.

That night, when I left the Savin compound, I asked Ivy, the only person I could trust, for help.

Ivy gathered my backpacks lying concealed across the cities, bags holding everything I may need if I ever had to run. With a new car, it was time for me to leave the life I had loved.

As I traveled, I started feeling sick, my stomach aching, and deeply nauseous. I assumed it was my stress from the previous days, but when I got to San Diego, it didn't stop.

That's when it hit me. Those nights with Dmitri had ended with him filling me up with his cum. I was so wrapped up in the man that I'd lost all sense of responsibility.

I quickly ran to a drugstore and bought a pregnancy test. When it was positive, I went back and bought four more, deciding to find a doctor when they were all positive. Ivy used her contacts here in California to help me.

Before this, I was not sure if I even wanted kids. Being so focused on my career and securing my leadership role in the cartel, having children wasn't something I'd ever thought of. All of a sudden, I found myself running from both the cartel and the Bratva with a big belly.

This baby boy may not have been what I'd planned or expected, but he is the best thing I've done. Demyan Savin is my life now. I live to protect him and keep him safe.

I didn't know if Dmitri was alive for the first few weeks. The Savin family had been hushed about the situation. But I heard from a source that he was back home recovering from surgery. Those weeks of not knowing if I had killed my son's father made me sad.

I would lie in bed crying, not knowing what day it was each time I awoke.

I touch my lips, thinking about him, sighing, and wiping a tear from my cheek.

Sitting in my reading chair, I stare at the precious baby in my arms. He has the Savin brothers' eyes. Even at a few weeks old, he looks like his father, and it sometimes brings me to tears to look at a child who reminds me of a love lost.

How can something that makes me happy also make me sad? Crying, I kiss my Savin baby.

Picking up my phone, I call Alexis. Her phone rings a few times before it hangs up. She refuses to take my calls.

I did what I could to protect her. Now, she has chosen to be on her own.

Chapter Thirty

DMITRI

I've lost something I never knew I wanted, Elise being the only woman I loved.

Sometime after that night, I woke up in a bed alone, hooked up to medical equipment, sighing in pain. My journey to recovery was long, spending too much time in seclusion thinking about her. I used my shoulder to take additional time to mend my heart before starting my new Brigadier role.

When I told her to run, I didn't want her to leave.

But I was crossed between my family and the woman I love. Not wanting my brother Nikolai to hurt her, I told her to run. At least then, she had a chance to survive. The cartel would be after her when they found me alive, but I knew Elise and that she would have a plan. She had planned for an escape in case of an emergency.

I had a choice to make that day, love or loyalty, and I chose my family. I'm not the kind of man who admits when he's wrong, but every day since then, I've held myself accountable for my bad decision.

Didn't I promise Elise, I would protect her? Still, I'd also promised my father that I'd always choose my brothers before anyone and everything, a promise I've always kept. But, thinking back on that day, maybe there was a way I didn't have to choose. Decisions are not always black and white. There's always another way. I just needed to figure out what that was. I was a coward. Faced with feelings I've never felt before, I chose the easy way out, my family.

I sent my men to her apartment, left trashed by the cartel. Underneath her pile of books and clothes, my men found a piece of jewelry on the floor. But that was months ago. She is gone, and that chapter in my life is over. I look down at the heart-shaped pendant in my hand.

But they also found a picture of Elise as a little girl, sitting on the beach with a girl a few years younger than her. I dug into her file and found that she has a sister, Alexis Walsh.

I've been trying to track her, hoping she will lead me to Elise, but even her sister has disappeared. After her sixteenth birthday, she ceased to exist. With Elise's aid, Alexis Walsh must have been hidden under a new identity for her protection. So, I didn't find her either.

We're at war, and Elise is part of it. If she returned to New York, the cartel and the Italians would try to kill her. Deciding it was for her safety, I paused my search. Elise needed to stay hidden and still does. When I win the war, I'll find her.

Without Elise, I feel nothing, having slipped back into a familiar, dark place. The space in my heart filled with love for Elise is once again black and empty. So, now, I rage against the cartel. With Nikolai by my side, the Russian Mafia has filled the streets with their blood. I will not stop killing until thoughts of Elise no longer consume me. There is no mercy for those who stand in our way. New York City belongs to the Coalition.

The world is dead to me until Elise is in my arms again.

Chapter Thirty-One

ANDREI

When Elise led the cartel in the attack on my family, I was immensely angered by her actions. Although she worked for our enemy, I'd always admired her. She was young and intelligent, and I respected her work. She hadn't been raised in this life like Liam or us. No, she'd made this life for herself through her hard work. I admired that about Elise.

I had known about Dmitri and Elise since the night of the fundraiser when I saw them in the alley. Dmitri had been in Russia for the past three years, and I wasn't sure what kind of trouble he would get himself in. I figured my brother was being his usual self, just sticking his dick between a beautiful woman's legs, nothing more.

But it was Elise who had surprised me. I am fiercely loyal to my wife, but even in my moments of weakness, when I made advances toward Elise, she didn't react to me. That day, I hit Dmitri for accusing me of being interested in her. I thought I had hidden those thoughts from everyone, including myself.

What I had first assumed was a one-time thing between Dmitri and Elise was becoming more than anyone could have imagined.

I confided in Nikolai about the ordeal. He insisted that a night in Russia would make Dmitri forget about Elise, but it didn't work. He couldn't wait to come home and return to her, spending the night with her in Room 403.

That's when Nikolai decided this thing between the two of them needed to end. We were planning a war with the cartel, and Elise was part of that, whether Dmitri and I wanted to involve her or not.

I was shocked when Elise was the one who took the first shot, trying to kill my brother. The situation had become a lot more complicated than I expected.

A woman my brother had fallen in love with stood before us—the very same one I had longed for but couldn't have. Only a woman like Elise could come face to face with the Savin brothers after starting a war and walk out alive.

My brother and I could never have foreseen that this woman would make us forget who we were, ruthless Bratva men, because all we had ever shown her was admiration and love.

My heart stopped when my brother pulled the trigger, then exhaled a sigh of relief when the gun was empty. My brother must have known he was out of bullets. At least, I hoped so.

When I saw the two of them together, I finally realized they were in love. My brother had never loved anyone besides himself before, and Elise had been the woman who had captured his heart.

For those few weeks, he had Elise in his heart, there was a change in him. He was starting to become the man I knew he could be. I had been waiting for my brother to move from being my shadow and become a leader of this family. That was hard for him growing up. Everyone, including him, had looked up to me to lead the Savins after our father's death. But he had the potential to lead beside me, not under me. I just needed him to see that.

I thought maybe his new role as Brigadier motivated the change, but I now know it was Elise. Since she's been gone, the man who'd emerged during that time has faded back into the shadows. Dmitri and Nikolai have rained the city's streets crimson with cartel and Italian blood.

We Savins didn't start the war, but we are winning it.

But, as Pakhan, I need to protect the Coalition. My brothers are out of control and becoming too careless. Separately, they create chaos. Together, they make their own hell. As the leader of this family and the Coalition, it's time I reined the two of them in, time for me to intervene.

So, I've called a family meeting.

Chapter Thirty-Two

DMITRI

Andrei sits behind his big desk, puffing on his cigar. He blows the smoke toward us as he sits patiently and quietly. Nikolai and I know we're in trouble. We came to the meeting expecting a scolding, but he didn't give us one.

"This war is taking many lives. We're going to need help." Andrei nods at his men to open the office door. A familiar man walks in, arms open.

"Anton!" Both Nikolai and I stand and greet our brother. We know his twin, Alexi, is doing recon work in Europe and won't be joining us. He's been gathering intel on the Italians. After greetings, Anton pulls up a chair next to us. Silence falls in the room as we wait for Andrei to continue.

"I've asked Anton to do something for me," says Andrei.

Anton hands a tablet to Andrei, who reviews its contents carefully before leaning back in his chair before handing it to me.

I scroll through pictures of a beautiful woman with brown hair and highlights flowing down her back, walking on the beach.

"Why did you look for her?" The woman I'm trying to forget is now on the screen in front of me. "You wasted your time." I throw the tablet at Nikolai, who scrolls through the pictures.

He sits there, legs sprawled out, arms around his neck, and laughs. "You sure, brother? I haven't seen you get any pussy action these past eight months. Thought you missed the bitch."

I grit my teeth, and Nikolai rolls his eyes at me. He knows he's out of line, even if he won't admit it.

Andrei grabs the tablet and looks at the pictures again. "Her sister, Alexis Walsh?" he asks our brother. He was also hoping her sister would lead us to Elise sooner.

"No trace of her," Anton says, emotionless. He doesn't know Elise like Andrei and I do. Personally, Anton doesn't care about her but he's our brother, and if she's important to us, she's important to him too.

"My search came up empty as well. No sign of her," I add.

"Elise is smart. She knew everyone would look for her. Let us hope the cartel doesn't have her." Andrei still puffs on his cigar, wrinkling his nose. This ordeal with the cartel and the Italian Mob has not been good for his first few months as Pakhan.

"Where is she?" I ask Anton.

"San Diego. Lives in a condo on Mission Beach." I'm surprised. Why didn't she leave the country? She's smart enough to know the U.S. wouldn't be safe, so why did she stop running?

"Is she alone?" I take another look at her pictures. Something about her has changed.

"Not quite." Both Andrei and I stop what we're doing to listen to our brother. Jealousy begins to rage within me.

Nikolai starts laughing and leans forward, putting his elbows on his knees as if about to hear some good gossip.

"What the fuck does that mean?" I'm growing impatient.

"Look more closely at the pictures. She's holding something." Anton points to a blanket she's clutching.

"And?" I study the picture more closely.

Anton's eyes dart to Andrei. "She has a baby with her. A baby boy." He pauses. "A boy with black hair and hazel eyes."

Those words knock every huff of air out of me. I sit speechless and confused. *I have a son!*

Anton adds, "Our men have informed me the cartel's found her. They're watching her right now as well."

This news worries me. If the cartel gets hold of Elise, she and my son will die a painful death.

Andrei stands up and places his hand on my shoulder. I find comfort in it. Right now, I need my big brother, not the Pakhan.

He gives Nikolai the order. "Get the plane ready. We're heading to California. Let's bring our nephew home before the cartel gets him."

As Nikolai walks out the door, he stops next to Andrei, whispering, "Did you find her for our brother or yourself?" Before Andrei can answer, Nikolai exits the room. I don't care about Andrei's reasons anyway. Right now, if I want to save Elise, I need all my brothers.

I stare at her picture, lost in thoughts. The love of my life is in danger because of me. I told her to run but should have held her in my arms and protected her against everything.

Hazel eyes. I can't see his face, but if he looks like his mother, I already know he's beautiful. My son, the future brigadier. *My son.* I never thought I'd say those words.

Fighting back the tears that form in the corner of my eye, I run my fingers along her picture, hoping I'm not too late.

If I get to them and save them, I'll never let them go.

I won't fail Elise again.

Chapter Thirty-Three

ELISE

Today is Demyan's six-week check-up. The doctor says he's healthy and growing well. We plan to see him again in a few weeks. As I hold Demyan, each day seems filled with a new, brighter glow. Still, I'm filled with dread thinking about the past and how it could affect my son.

I try not to leave the condo unless necessary. Since I needed to take Demyan to the doctor's, I stopped at the store to get diapers and some groceries and then made a quick trip to the coffee shop. I'm arriving home later than expected.

My phone rings with a private number. Only Ivy and Amelia have my contact information, but the knot in my stomach tells me to answer it.

"Hello," I answer nervously. The other side of the line is quiet for a few seconds.

"Elise," says the deep voice. *Liam!*

"Elise, run!" he shouts.

"What? How did you find me?" I ask.

"My father knows where you are. He's sent some men to get you. If he catches you, you'll be taken straight to Mexico. Run!"

The phone clicks, and then there's nothing.

Chills run down my body, and my heart starts pounding out of my chest. My steps become longer as I hurry home. Protecting Demyan is all I can think of. If Señor Martinez knows Demyan is a Savin, he will be cruel to a baby, even if it's innocent.

As I approach my condo building, I glance to my left and notice a nicely dressed man leaning against the car. I can't make out his face yet, but something about him is familiar. He puffs his cigarette, throwing the butt on the ground before squishing it with his black boots.

"Hola, Elise," he says with a wicked grin.

"Erik," I gasp. Erik Martinez is Liam's brother, who runs the cartel operations out of Los Angeles. I knew I was close to him, but he doesn't usually come to San Diego because it's too hot for the FBI and DEA with border control so close.

Tightening my grip on the stroller, I scurry across the street toward the building elevators. He doesn't run after me. He doesn't have to.

Quickly, I press the elevator button, watching the panel as it shows each floor it travels on its way to me. Two men start down the hallway in my direction. When the door opens, I push the stroller in and press the 'close door' button as fast as possible.

A sigh escapes as the door begins to close, but a hand appears, preventing it from closing. With my heeled boots, I kick the hand, aiming for his knuckles as I hear a "fucking bitch," and he lets the door go.

Demyan starts to stir from his sleep, and I rock the stroller with my leg. One more floor until the ding sounds as the door opens.

I quickly round the corner, ready for a fight. Not seeing anyone, I grab the stroller and walk down the hall. A man suddenly appears at the end as I unlock my front door. He starts to march toward me angrily as I slam the door in his face, locking it.

Inside, the lights aren't on. I always keep them on, but I left when the sun was still out, so maybe I forgot today. I turn off the alarm and try to turn on the light, but it doesn't come on.

There are five deadbolts, and I run my hands along the door, feeling for them in the dark and making sure they're all secured. Then, my back leans against the door as I breathe heavily.

The man on the other side pounds on it, yelling curse words.

Demyan starts to fuss, so I fumble around his stroller and try to get him out. "Mama's got you. Hold on." Grabbing him, I curl him in my arms, leaning his head on my chest, taking a moment to think about my next move.

The pounding on the door gets louder, and the man forcefully tries to kick my door down. Retreating from the door further into my apartment, I'm stopped by suddenly feeling my back against someone. A hand wraps around my mouth. I attempt to scream, but no one would hear.

I pull Demyan closer into my arms, unable to say anything else. My hands tremble, and my heart beats faster.

"I told you, you're mine. You belong to me," the man whispers in my ear.

Before I can react, my door bursts open to a cartel man standing in my doorway, gun in hand. He lifts his arm to shoot, a bang rippling through the air.

My body goes blank from fear that I've been shot, but I'm snapped back when the man in front of me drops, blood spreading on my carpet.

Standing directly behind him is a Russian man. *Andrei.*

The hand over my mouth releases, and the light flicks on. I quickly look in that direction and see a shadow. "Dmitri!"

There's another round of gunshots, and we look to see Nikolai leaving a few dead cartel bodies in my hallway.

Andrei and Nikolai enter, blocking the door so there's no escape.

The last time I saw these men, I tried to kill them. The Savin brothers don't forgive those who cause them harm. With their new status in the Coalition, the Savin brothers are now among the most feared families in the underground world.

"My son, I presume?" Dmitri's eyes are focused on Demyan.

"Yes," I respond in a faltering voice, scared. But my fear is different now; I'm more worried about the little boy I'm holding in my arms than I am about my own life.

"Did you name him?" He leans in to get a closer look at the baby.

"Yes." I swallow a lump in my throat.

"So, what is it?" His question is harsh, as though he's interrogating me.

"Demyan," I answer. Demyan was their grandfather's name. I remembered it from when I did my research on the Savin family. The rumors were that he was a genius, so it was the perfect name for the son of two intellectual individuals.

A hint of a smile appears on his face, then quickly fades away. "Did you know you were carrying our son when you tried to kill me?" Dmitri takes a step closer.

"No," I answer honestly.

"He's a Savin, Elise." His eyes never leave the baby.

"I know who he is." I'm reminded every day when I look into my baby's almost hazel eyes.

"Then you know he belongs in New York with my family and me." His brothers step forward and circle me.

"Dmitri!" I start sobbing and move further away from him, holding Demyan tight, unwilling to let him take him.

"I'm sure you already know I'm Brigadier now." His cold eyes move to mine.

"I know." I haven't seen him in months and don't know if the man standing in front of me is the same one I fell in love with.

"The cartel wants you dead, Elise." Andrei moves closer, and I start to feel suffocated by their presence.

"Obviously." The dead cartel men still lie on the ground.

How could I think it was possible to make this my home? I should have kept running. Why did I stop?

"So, you know it's not safe for my son to be here where they can find him." Dmitri keeps stepping closer, his eyes darting back and forth from me to his son.

"He's, my son. I won't let you take him." I pull the blanket over Demyan's face to shield him.

"Elise, I came to take my son home. He'll be the next Brigadier. He needs to be in New York and be prepared to take my seat when the time comes," Dmitri growls.

"No, Dmitri. You can't take him away from me."

Dmitri moves toward me. With every step he takes, I step backward toward Andrei and Nikolai.

I pull Demyan closer and hold him as tight as I can. He starts to cry.

"Dmitri! Please. I'm his mother!" I shout as tears fall down my cheeks. I continue to get away from Dmitri until my body hits a hard chest.

Dmitri now pins me against Andrei, both so close I feel their bodies on mine, trapping me between two Savin brothers so I cannot escape.

Dmitri rubs my lips with his fingers, parting them before leaning in and kissing me. My body relaxes, and my mind goes wild. One touch from him, and I'm falling hard for him as though it's the first time again.

Goosebumps form as Andrei breathes on my neck.

Looking at Demyan, Dmitri replies to my plea, "I know. That's why you're going home with us."

Shock hits me. *They want me home with them.*

I hear Nikolai say, "You sure about this?"

I turn my head to Andrei. As he's looking down at me, I find the face of an old friend. "She's one of us now, whether you like it or not."

Chapter Thirty-Four

ELISE

It's been a month since Dmitri found me in San Diego. Sitting at the table, I look over at him, gushing. Today is one of the happiest days of my life.

He smiles back at me. "Hi, Mrs. Savin."

The love I have for this man, my man, is deep and internal. For the first time, I'm encouraged to feel and share rather than having to put on a front.

He grabs my hand, and I feel as though I'm home.

I'm right where I need to be here with Dmitri and Demyan. Together, we can achieve the strength and stability none of us can attain alone.

Andrei raises his wine glass in the air as we hush to hear him. "Congratulations, Mr. and Mrs. Savin," he toasts. Everyone at the table raises their glasses and cheers.

We are celebrating with a Savin family dinner tonight. Today, I became Dmitri's wife, who will hold his heart until we drown in our own crimson blood.

No longer part of the cartel, the Savin family welcomed me into their home and family. However, Nikolai still watches me, untrusting. I've been moving with caution around him and hope I'll earn his trust with time.

I belong to Dmitri now, and I'm good with that. I'm also safe as long as he's by my side.

Andrei continues, "Welcome to the family, Elise. There were some complications before, but now, all that is forgotten." Nikolai scowls, and I immediately notice Dmitri glancing his way.

Andrei continues, "You are officially a Savin. Because of that, I want to give you a wedding gift I believe you deserve. Beginning now, Elise Savin, you are officially the Chief Financial Officer of the Savin businesses, working alongside Dmitri and me to increase the family fortune."

Cora and Mrs. Savin are ecstatic about the news, but the moment is cut short.

Dmitri immediately declines. "No. She is my wife and my son's mother. I must protect her."

Andrei agrees, "Yes, brother. That's why she will operate solely under our legitimate businesses. We will not include her in Coalition affairs for now." *For now*, I think. The thought of standing by the Pakhan's side excites me.

Dmitri can see the excitement on my face. I am so happy to be returning to work. I love being Demyan's mom, but I also love my career. I've missed that these past months. Not wanting to disappoint me, Dmitri reluctantly agrees.

"Thank you," I silently mouth to him.

"I love you." I want to hear those words every day for the rest of my life.

"I love you, too," I reply, staring into the face no longer hardened but full of affection for me.

Our moment is cut short. Suddenly, the house shakes, and a window in the next room shatters, sending shards of glass everywhere. I instinctively jump to Demyan, sitting on Dmitri's lap, and grab him. The men stand up, guns in hand, and start flying rounds.

I'm no longer part of this fight. The last time I was here, I was the one firing bullets, but I have my son now. I shield him, hiding in the corner of the room with Cora and the future Pakhan.

The men leave the room, but I can still hear them shouting and fighting. The noise becomes distant, leaving me with a crying baby in my arms.

Footsteps approach, and I immediately draw my gun, finding Alejandro and I staring at each other, guns pointed at one another. I dart my eyes to Demyan, still in my arms.

I'm willing to sacrifice my life to protect my son. I wouldn't think twice about putting a bullet in Alejandro, someone I trusted with my own life at one time.

He lowers his weapon. "Elise, Liam gave specific orders to keep you and your son alive."

Surprised by the comment, I ask, "Why?"

"Because he needs you. You're part of his plan."

He hands me an envelope before a whistling sound pervades. Alejandro drops a few feet from me, dying on the ground, blood gurgling, then spewing from his lips.

Nikolai stands next to us, his pistol still pointed at the dead man.

Demyan starts to scream, and I pull him deeper into my chest.

I look at the envelope to see it addressed to *'My dearest Elise.'*

A NOTE FROM THE AUTHOR

Thank you for reading my book.
I hope you loved reading my story as much as I enjoyed writing it.
Your support means a lot to me. Thank you!
Shana

CONTINUE READING

Want more sinfully dangerous Bratva stories? Keep reading now!

A LOVE THAT BLEEDS